The Andy Project

Kathy Trithardt

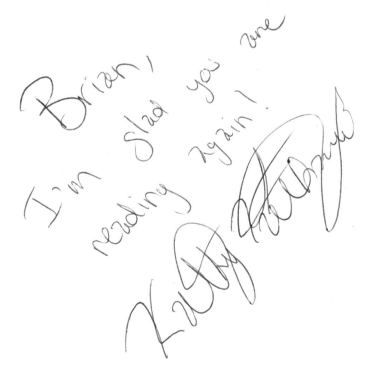

Brian,
I'm glad you are
reading again!
Kathy Trithardt

All characters and events in this publication are fictitious and any
resemblance to "actual" persons, living or dead, it purely luck and
coincidence. If you see yourself in a character, it doesn't mean you
are the same person, unless you are also fictional – which would
make for a really fun tale.

theonlykathytrithardt.wordpress.com

ISBN 9781494831073

The author photo was taken by Taylor Lewis.
It was taken, unbeknownst to the subject, in a moment of people
watching glee in Victoria, BC.

They say you can tell a lot about whether or not a book is going to be any good by reading the first sentence; the problem with that method is that I just don't know how to judge anything I write. For that matter, I don't know if I am judging what other people write using a critical eye, either. I usually just read the piece all the way through and decide how it made me feel. Maybe my lack of eye for what is considered good or bad is what has held me back in the past. It would probably be easier to toss out lots of different reasons why this is the first time I am doing this, so I'm not putting too much focus in one place, as I believe I would be doing so erroneously.

I might be getting ahead of myself. I'm not entirely sure how this process is supposed to happen, besides the notion that I am meant to keep writing, and to do that I needed to have begun. I guess this is as good a start as any. At least, taking a running leap into writing is what my therapist recommended, and I believe I am ready to give this a try. The worst thing that will happen is I spend a lot of time making something that will eventually be used as fire starter, if it is ever printed, and doesn't just remain as a digital file on my laptop.

Although it seems strange to introduce myself to what is essentially just myself, I'm going to do it anyway. I have no one in my life that will likely have any interest in reading this - I am not writing for an audience outside of my own mind. Introductions come at the beginning, so I just want to be clear. I'm Andy. My name isn't even technically Andrew, like most people named Andy. Just Andy. I looked it up once, and it means "manly" - which makes me picture a rugged woodsman bringing home something he had hunted himself. "Manly" has always brought forth mental images of tough, outdoorsy, bearded men who enjoy hearty foods and mugs of ale. I don't even really like camping all that much, let alone mugs of anything stronger than coffee, and I look terrible when I neglect my shaving routine.

Perhaps when my parents were deciding how to name me, they envisioned that I would be a fun-loving, outgoing super star implied by a shortened nickname; I've met several other Andys and they seem to fit this pattern better than I ever have. Evidently my parents decided to just skip the stoic manifestations of being called Andrew in order to thrust me into a fun personality type. Andrew sounds more dignified or professional than the shortened counterpart. Ironically, Andrew probably suits how people think about me better than my actual name, but I like Andy anyway. I've grown pretty used to my name, as people tend to do. I don't walk around with a snotty nose in the air, but I do get a hell of a lot of work done.

Before I come off as a complete bore, it is important to note that I do like to have fun; I just do it on a much smaller scale than the stereotype with which I have become familiar for someone called Andy. It is amazing how many people automatically assume that I want to party, until they learn what I do for a living: finance. Yes, it is as boring as it sounds, but someone has to do it. It also pays pretty decently and is dependable work, so I've stuck to it because it is easy for me. I have no problem working through the numbers. The problem is that I gave up the dream of one day creating something with words instead of numbers a long time ago; what is harder than admitting that problem is actually following through with that dream, years later, of creating something outside of me that is tangible and worth existing. It is hard to get started on something I have placed so high on a pedestal. If I start but then never finish writing at least one novel, I'll feel like I've failed and the dream dies. The terrifying paradox is that if I never try, I never have the chance to have done it.

So, here I am, 32 years old, taking a chance. I think that if I just start writing, I might be able to salvage something that comes out on the page and turn it into something brilliant. Until that happens, I'm going to keep writing about what is going on in my life. I don't know how inspiring it will be, but I have to start somewhere. I'm not used to putting words on the page. I heard some advice once that basically said to start by writing one letter, turn that letter into a word, turn that word into a sentence, turn that sentence into a paragraph, turn that paragraph into a chapter and turn that chapter into a novel. That makes it sound so easy. I guess the mechanics of it are easy, if you look at it with that simplified logic, but it is hard to believe that it will be simple.

Another piece of advice I have heard over and over is that you should write what you know; I happen to know way too much about the finance world, but even thinking about writing it, let alone having anyone read it, makes me think of falling asleep, so I refuse to use that bank of knowledge. I will, instead, write about things I observe on a day-to-day basis, and things I have experienced in the past. I've always been a fan of standing on the side lines and watching the players in our world; what makes them talk the way they do, dress the way they do, think the way they do? I've caught myself watching interactions and just enjoying other people's moments as they unfold around me. If I am very still, no one even notices that I'm there. The thrill of capturing magical moments, even if they are moments that would seem mundane to the person experiencing them, is a hobby I have always had, and it is one that I believe will give me some resources to fill this project with interesting ideas.

I am really getting to know myself lately, which is partly to do with the aforementioned therapist. I want to kick my own butt for how lame that sentence sounds, but I don't exactly have a reputation to uphold. I'm becoming more comfortable with the idea that asking for help doesn't mean there is anything wrong with you, but, rather, the opposite. A few months back I realized that I've gotten myself into a slump, and haven't been very happy. It was bordering on being a deep depression, and I couldn't really explain why. There's nothing particularly terrible going on in my life, but this irksome feeling kept creeping up, and I couldn't help but feel sad, as though the routine I have worked to keep constant is no longer sufficient. I want something more - and upon reflection it seems like I've been hoping for something more to come along for a really long time, but nothing has presented itself to me. I've learned with Dr. Macaw's help that even though I am perceived as just a boring numbers guy, who has little of interest to say in social settings because he spends all his time working through figures, I am not my job. It is what I do, not who I am. It is also up to me to influence my world and seek out areas of interest instead of waiting for them to make themselves known.

3

When I was a kid, I loved learning but hated school; I always wanted to do something less structured, more creative, and for a brief time I was kind of the class clown, pain in the butt kid who fought against the all rules because I found them restrictive and boring. Eventually, I could see the look of panic and fear in my parents' eyes - their only son was going to spend all his time trying to be somebody who could not survive without a spotlight, somebody who relied on his clowning as a way to get through life, and would no doubt struggle to make ends meet because the world wouldn't take him seriously. I could physically feel their fear of having to support me for the rest of my life unless I did something profitable instead of amusing myself. They pushed me into working with numbers, and since I realized that I'm good at them, I didn't put up much of a struggle after the first few shoves. I couldn't risk completely disappointing my parents, and they were always incredibly upset when I got in trouble for going against my teachers. I wanted them to be proud of me, and they were never thrilled by my creative outbursts.

If I ever finish a book, I hope they will be proud of me when I hand it to them. I don't even mean in a published format - I would just print it out, put it in a binder and hand it to them. I don't know if they would even stop to consider the fact that I have that potential creativity hiding in me that could co-exist with the structured destiny they had in mind for me.

I'm not giving up my job to do this project – far from it. This project is for my own personal benefit, and I'm going to prove that I can do it in my spare time, instead of sitting around feeling as though something is missing from my life. I want to make this project a priority because it means something to me, something I will eventually find the adequate words to describe. The Doc said something about letting my creative side flourish, but that doesn't feel like it really covers it. Sure, I want to let that side of myself out of the box that I have kept it in - in my imagination, it hides in a shoebox under my parents' bed, like a toy that was taken away because I misbehaved. I've declared my punishment over, and I'm taking back what belongs to me.

There is another aspect of my current existence that has been called into question during my sessions with Mr. Macaw: relationships. I've had a handful of romantic relationships throughout my adult life, but I'm pretty awkward when it comes to women. I'm quiet, and have been accused of being distant, and while I've tried to convey the excitement of anything I've succeeded in at work to women I've dated, I sense boredom behind their glossy eyes. They don't follow what I am talking about, even when I feel like I am breaking it down to simple terms, and over the years I have learned to just give up on trying to explain it. Someone once told me I sounded condescending when I tried to simplify the story without losing the amusement. I didn't want anyone to think I was talking down to them, so eventually an entire five minute story would get reduced to, "I had a good day at work." Sometimes the woman I was seeing at the time would ask why, but I soon learned it was best to not even bother trying to explain any more.

I don't currently have anyone in my life. Although I miss companionship, the wayward affection of my cat Figaro and my internet search history on my personal laptop have kept me mostly satisfied. I don't really have many friends - none that I see on a regular basis, anyway. I don't go out all that much, because I am comfortable at home. Perhaps this writing project will help to get me out of that comfort zone, but I don't see any problem in being alone. I'm not depriving anyone the pleasure of my presence. If I had someone to be with, I'd be there, but my social calendar has grown dusty and I haven't found the motivation to shake off the cobwebs.

***

Something I have always done, but rarely reflected on, is delight in people watching. I enjoy witnessing intriguing moments in the lives of strangers. Sometimes they are kids who say adorable things in the seat behind me on the bus, or people walking down the street who are caught up in their own world. I love seeing glimpses into people's personal worlds. I'll try to report on any that happen while I am putting these words onto digital paper.

There is a woman I see from time to time that catches my eye and holds my attention. She is a magnificent giraffe of a woman - although I can only assume she'd find offense in that description if she heard it without the full context. She is tall and slender, with beautifully wide eyes that are only slightly obscured by her glasses. She dresses modestly but always in well-fit clothing, as though everything she has was made for exactly her. For all I know, it is, as I know some tall people shop at specialty stores or have to have everything they purchase altered so it doesn't look like they have gone through a growth spurt since dressing themselves that morning. Every time I see her, she embodies grace; I've noticed her quite a few times while she's been off in her own little world, working through things in her head, and it is a delight to see her in her natural habitat. I'm discreet when I watch her - and I don't follow her around or anything strange. I just observe her when she is in the same space as me, because I am drawn to do so. Perhaps she could serve as a muse for this project, since her life seems much more fascinating than what I have been able to offer to people who acted on their curiosity toward me. I see her most often in the lobby of the building where I work; the building is shared by several different offices, so I can only guess as to which one she reports. She always seems to sit off to the side when I do see her in the lobby, with a large cup of coffee in hand, looking over thick binders and struggling to pull her curly, deep brown hair back out of her eyes when it falls in her face. I heard someone, I assume a colleague, try to get her attention from across the lobby by calling her name: Gabriella. Her name is truly gorgeous, and fits her stature, beauty, and nature perfectly. If I were a more confident man, and if I had anything more interesting to say to her than anything to do with finance, I would love to speak to her. I feel like her end of the conversation would be deep, robust and interesting, and I just want to drink that in.

Of course, this is all in my head, but it is what I have observed, and what my instincts tell me. I haven't allowed myself to really think about whether or not this could turn into a real life physical attraction. I've had a lot of disappointment in that department, and sometimes it just feels better to let fantasy prevail.

Something else that has stopped me from working on a writing project in the past is that even though I would love to write a novel, I haven't been satisfied with any of the plots that have formed in my mind. I always find huge holes and imperfections, get frustrated and just give up on it before I even start writing it down. I wouldn't want to propose this dream but do it badly. I ache to finish something of which I can be proud.

***

I was contemplating my commute today. I wake up on a floor high above the street, shit, shower and shave, get dressed, occasionally remember to eat breakfast. I then take the stairs down to the ground level, as the elevator is ancient and maddeningly slow, so only useful when transporting heavy loads. It also scares the bejesus out of Figaro, so if I ever have to take him to the vet, he makes me carry his travel box up and down the stairs. Sometimes I stop in for a coffee at a little place close to my bus stop, but that usually depends on whether or not I bothered with breakfast. I take the bus 12 stops toward downtown, and then go into another building and to a floor with a number even higher than the one on which I awoke. I go about my day, dancing with digits, refuelling my body once it realizes it is hungry. I do the same commute in reverse, but almost never go to the coffee shop on my way home. I think I am happiest when I am closer to the ground. It's not that I have a fear of heights, but rather that I feel more as though I am in the middle of something of which I am a part, instead of being trapped in a box suspended above the people going about their day. Although I prefer my apartment to my time in the office, I sometimes get the same feeling if I have stayed inside too long and it only goes away after a lengthy walk outside. It might be that I require the fresh air, or the movement, or even being closer to other people, even if it is to just observe their manners, habits and interactions. I'm not sure, but even though I am happy being by myself, I crave this injection into the world from time to time. It is as though the whole world just flows around me, like weightless water. I sometimes enjoy my journey more when it is raining, even though the thought of leaving the warmth and comfort of my home to walk in the rain always seems bothersome. It is right up there with not wanting to get out of bed because the temperature outside of the covers is nowhere near as soothing and enticing as the heated pit underneath the blankets.

I see these two particular children and their mother on my bus most days. I'm not great with guessing ages, but I would say the little boy is around 5 years old, and the little girl is around 8 years old. The sister takes really good care of her brother, keeping him amused on the bus by playing games, such as counting cars. She always gives up the window seat for him, even though you can tell that she would like to sit there, at least once in a while. Their mother sits across the aisle, oblivious to her kids' actions. She is clearly not a morning person. She dresses for warmth and comfort, but her kids are always well dressed. She ties her hair back out of her face, and always seems to have her nose in her phone. I don't want to make any speculations as to who she is talking to. Perhaps no one. She might just be playing a game for all I know. I think she uses this time as her own personal respite. Her daughter takes care of her son and gives her five minutes of peace while they are in the safety of the bus, and she doesn't have to worry about them. The mother always holds the son's hand when they get off the bus, and usually helps him disembark by picking him up and depositing him safely on the sidewalk. The children always thank the bus driver with gusto.

The first time I saw this trio, I jumped to a judgement about how she was ignoring her kids, but I think this updated view is closer to the truth of the matter. She puts most of her energy into getting her children clothed, fed, and onwards to school and just takes a tiny moment during transit to breathe and be distracted. I've grown to admire her, as she is raising two really polite kids, and I can already tell the little girl is bright.

That's what I really enjoy about this transit route - things change, but perceptions of constants change over time as well. I feel like each day I get another piece of the puzzle belonging to the people I observe. If I collect another puzzle piece, I am a step closer to being able to immortalize a character similar to each of these people in my writing. I just have to figure out where they fit, or see what kind of story they want to tell. I guess I have already told a snip of her story as I've grown to observe it, even if it didn't follow a traditional beginning, middle and end format.

***

It happened again. I got caught up in just submerging myself in a marathon of crime shows on tv, and now it is the middle of the night - better described as early morning - but I can't seem to go to sleep. Even Figaro cannot seem to keep up with my crime show marathon antics, and wandered out of the room several times, only to come back every couple of episodes to retrieve a sneaky cuddle. I must have told myself several times, "just one more episode," before I gave up thinking about the time. It doesn't help that there isn't much of a break between one episode and the next. Just when you are looking for the remote to turn off the television, the next opening pops up and drags you into the next storyline. I always figure I'll quit after they set up the case of the week, but they are all so intriguing. I suppose the writers are doing their job and hooking their audience, but it makes for sleepless nights when they are put on the station back to back. I suppose it would be even worse if they played the episodes in order, as you'd start to focus even more on the secondary plot lines.

I like to indulge in watching fiction, because I get wrapped up in the characters, the stories and the different places around this world (or others) that the plots jump around, but doing it in giant bursts always makes me feel guilty that I wasn't more productive. Any time frame where Figaro seems to be beating me on the productivity scale is a worry to me, since the only things on his schedule are finding patches of sunshine and bathing or napping in them. I've neglected working on the project (hell, I haven't even starting writing my novel, but at least I am putting words into this pseudo journal), but had several hours to use in watching reruns (although I hadn't previously seen that many of the episodes I watched, to be fair). I could consider it research, but a small part of me feels like that is a cop out. The fine details of the characters in those shows always disappear from my mind by the next time a case comes around, indicated by a new episode.

I guess watching the show was less about having to be productive and more about relaxing, which is something with which I have a strange relationship. I enjoy relaxing when it is happening; I look forward to it when I haven't relaxed in a while, and it is good to spend quality time with Figaro, even though he doesn't seem to really care one way or the other as long as I keep his bowl full, but I have a sort of pessimistic view as to figuring out when I'll be allowed to take relaxations breaks again. After relaxing, I sometimes feel guilty, like right now, which is why instead of going to sleep, like I should have done several hours ago, I am adding words to this project in the hope that I can kill the guilt long enough to get back to a state in which I am relaxed and can sleep peacefully. I'm just glad I didn't try to "relax" on a night where I work the next morning, although I'm sure the guys at the office would just pat me on the back with a knowing smile of "oh yeah, I bet you partied hard last night". I've never been hungover at work before in my life, and yet it would be okay with them, because my name is Andy. We live in a world of very strange rules. I'm pretty sure my cat wouldn't see any difference in me, either.

It is such a paradox. From my discussions with Dr. Macaw, I gather that I'm just not all that accustomed to spending time on myself. When I heard that, it sounded ridiculous - I'm "with" myself all the time, so I must spend all my time on myself! Fortunately, I soon began to see why that was wrong. Like many adults, I have a job that I attend out of duty and need for income but am not particularly amused by - it has its moments - so although I get the promised pay cheque every other week, I am essentially selling my time. The time I spend at the office (and sometimes the time I spend worrying about the office or getting to the office when I know the day is going to be chaotic) is time that is directed anywhere but toward my own behalf. A lot of my energy is directed specifically outside of myself for work purposes. This makes sense - nearly everyone has to work - but it shouldn't be as significant of a drain on my brain, or I should at least have a way of recharging my brain that meets my need for efficiency.

I'm not saying there is anything wrong with directing a lot of energy into one's work. We all have to work and make a living. It is just wrong for me to think that I am spending any of that time on myself - at least in the current way I do things. Sometimes I don't even stop to take breaks, because I feel like I will get the work done faster and better if I don't distract myself with a trip to the lobby to stretch my legs or a break for lunch. In that, I am actively ignoring what I do need, and specifically not spending time on myself as a cost to get my work completed. I almost never leave work early, despite giving up the multitude of moments that I could take during the day but choose not to. I don't know how many times I have arrived home to realize I hadn't had more than a cup of coffee on the way to work, and as fired up as my mind feels from the caffeine, it is not very nourishing.

I feel selfish taking time for myself (which my logical side realizes is really ridiculous considering I don't have many people in my life to whom I want to give my time), but I really just need to change the connotation of that word. I've always felt that being selfish was a negative, that only bad people do it, but it seems to me that if I bothered to tap into that selfishness every once in a while, I wouldn't feel the need to power through every project at work and leave no time to feed myself. I would eat, clear my head and be able to do my work with a better version of my mind. I wouldn't build up this sense of needing to keep ignoring my tiny, insignificant needs until they culminate in a marathon of crime shows, after which I feel horrible for indulging. I want to enjoy my relaxations - before, during *and* after! I'm decently sure that is what true relaxation must be like, instead of letting doubt and guilt creep in. I feel sheepish about putting myself on my schedule because it feels like a foreign concept. In theory, all the blank space on my schedule should be spent on myself, but it doesn't really work that way.

Working on this project is something else that I want to do (especially starting the fiction portion), and I want to schedule specifically to do it for myself, because this is for absolutely no one else. I've actually returned to a sense of calm while tossing down these words, instead of lying sleepless and wrapped up in my guilt that I had enjoyed some mind candy and now the excess sugar is keeping me from my sleep obligation. All thoughts of obligations need to stop - I should do things because I want to, not because I have to. I should go to the office and see it for what it is: a job. That doesn't mean I cannot enjoy myself within those walls. I've figured out that when I do take short breaks and go for a quick deli lunch or just sit in the lobby and people watch, I enjoy my day better. Even if I take a lunch of leftovers into the conference room and let the glass walls muffle the sounds of the chaos that bounce around the office, I am better able to just breath, remembering that I don't need to be there at all times to hold things together. My responsibilities are not so imperative that I cannot take time to taste, chew, swallow and ingest my lunch. The chaos will always been there, in one way or another, and although I play my part in trying to control it, it will be far worse for me and my coworkers if I let the chaos consume me instead of consuming my lunch.

On that note, I am going to brush my teeth and maybe even floss - activities I tend to skip if I have stayed up too late because my theory has always been that sleeping will get me more energy for the work I need to do, and I can always brush my teeth in the morning without anyone knowing I didn't do it before bed. I am going to make sure that I don't set any alarms for tomorrow morning, because I want to make tomorrow about myself, and I don't want to feel pressured into fitting in every possible item that could be crammed onto a schedule. I want to just enjoy taking time to do whatever fulfills me or makes me happy. I'll probably feel stupid about this idea once I wake up, and try to find something "productive" instead, but whatever I end up doing, I hope it is for myself, and not some outside force that doesn't acknowledge my acts as going above and beyond my duties.

As for the aspirations of writing a novel, maybe I'll start with a short novel. Somehow that makes it seem like less of a challenge - as though the addition of the word "short" takes most of the pressure off - and yet I won't have to stick to a short story format. I just want to get ideas down, create characters and see where they want to go. I just have to commit to making some choices as to who those characters are, and what they want.

***

Office parties that you are required to attend are the worst way I can think of spending my evening. I don't think it should even really be called a party, even though it involves appetizers and beverages. It is mostly just a meeting dressed up as a party, where we are expected to "get to know" our coworkers better through "fun" exercises, but it really just turns into people abusing the free alcohol, and since my name is Andy, and that clearly means I like to party, I get handed a drink with a slap on the back every time I set down my cup. Trying to refuse the offered beverage is always met with intense disapproval, as though I cannot exist in this situation outside of what is socially accepted. I kept carrying around a cup of cola, pretending it had alcohol in it if people asked what I was drinking, and had to make sure to keep refilling it when I accidently drained it, which happens when I'm at a loss of anything else to do. It felt pathetic to admit to myself that I would much rather leave early and get back home to my cat. I don't even like cola, but water doesn't fool anyone.

Although I like the idea of knowing more about the people I see on a daily basis, I don't feel like this is the way to do it. I would rather have a quiet meal with them and talk one-on-one, or even in a very small group, than have to stand up, attempt to keep my drink full at all times, wrangle with appetizers that are messier to eat than intended, and be singled out every time I just want to stand in the back corner where I can actually hear my own thoughts instead of whatever music is being blasted. Yelling over music in an attempt to "get to know" these people is of no help to me. I don't want to know them in a pressured social situation; I want to know the actual people they are, and I feel a more relaxed approach would be a better way to go about this.

We have these meetings every six months or so, and I tried to skip one once - but someone actually takes attendance and I got a call telling me how much fun I was missing, and pretty much insisting I take part unless I wanted to appear unfriendly. I find it easier just to not fight it, since no one seems to understand why I wouldn't want to get loaded on the company dime. I guess some people feel as though this "free" food and drink is a bonus that they have worked for, but I find it all incredibly awkward.

Maybe I'll put a suggestion in the box that we reallocate the money they spend on these parties to smaller meetings from time to time. It would take some logistical planning to figure out who knows each other already and who should be "partnered" with whom, but I would be more comfortable, and would actually enjoy getting to know these people instead of watching the clock and calculating how long until I will be allowed to leave without punishment. If only Figaro were a child instead of a cat, I'd have a great excuse, but then I would need a nanny to watch over him. Compared to offspring, Figaro is a pretty cheap and easy companion, so I can't place any blame on him for not getting me out of these functions.

***

Dr. Macaw suggested that I try to get a little bit more exercise into my day, which makes a lot of sense considering I spend most of my day bent over a desk. I've started making hourly excuses to get out of my chair and move a little bit, without making it obvious that I am taking these short breaks. I've made a little game of coming up with reasons to get up.

Sometimes I'll take my coffee cup to the staff kitchen area, as though I am getting a refill, but leave the same cold coffee in my cup, because I never have more than a cup unless it was a particularly bad sleep the night before.

Sometimes I will deliver paperwork to people, and sometimes I'll purposefully put it in the wrong place so I can move it when the next hour rolls around. I always make a point of putting on my "I'm clearly busy doing important work" face while I walk around, but internally, I am just enjoying the movement and the change of surroundings.

I find it is helping me clear my head, and even though my brain sometimes wanders, thinking about what I'll do when I take my next hourly walk, I feel like I have gotten more work finished in this past week than when I just plow through it, constantly chained to my desk. I've even made it a point to take my lunch break - and actually leave my desk to do so. This may or may not be influenced by my enjoyment of watching people in the lobby area more so than wanting to get some movement into my day, but I am learning to treasure this midday vacation. It also doesn't hurt that I am seeing more and more of Gabriella, although I doubt I'll ever actually strike up a conversation with her. It seems backwards to put it down, but I enjoy being attracted to her from afar. It is not so much that I want to take her to bed or anything, although I'm sure I would enjoy that if it were to happen; it is more to do with being attracted to her as an intriguing feature of my day-to-day life.

I feel like she would have amazing stories to tell, and that they would be much more interesting than what I would bring to the

16

conversation. I would rather picture her talking about her day than summon the courage to ask her about it, because I fear that by interacting with her, I might change her patterns, and I might not be able to observe her. If I were to come on too strong, or say the wrong thing, perhaps she would avoid me, and I would no longer be able to watch her from afar without disturbing her.

Of course this is all just in my head. Maybe we would have an excellent conversation, and we would be able to smile at each other when our paths cross, trading tidbits about our day. If I am ever able to give up the fear of having her presence taken out of my day by injecting myself into her life, I would love to just have lunch next to her and learn more about the woman who fascinates me.

I also worry that I have built her up to be a completely wonderful person, and it would blow my little world if that turned out to be wrong. I wouldn't be able to enjoy just noticing her existence anymore if she turned out to be less than I expect of her, and that is unfair on a few different levels.

Maybe I just need to shift my focus off her entirely and just observe on a more broad scale, rather than become dependant on the fantasy I am building around one woman who may or may not be as amazing as she is inside my head. I feel like I am overthinking this, and if anyone were to read this, they'd think I was obsessed. I wouldn't blame them; I sound obsessed.

I guess it is just hard to write about something, or someone, about whom I have limited knowledge, and not sound like I am repeating myself. Repetition is an indication of focus, focus is an indication of obsession. At least, that is how I think of it. Obsession doesn't have to be a bad thing, but when it comes to talking too much about people you hardly know (or only know inside your head), it tends to be taken in the negative.

The problem is there are only so many places from which I draw inspiration to even put down words, so I've found myself focussing my attention more intently to try to have something other than my "boring" job to talk about. Sure, I am amused by the little games I play to get myself moving around the office, but I'm not sure that makes for great novel subject matter unless I really up the ante and toss in some mysterious or possibly dangerous antics. I could try doing aerobics behind peoples' backs when no one is looking, and just try not to get caught doing it (although I'd like to mention that I am not currently trained to be a ninja, so any form of acrobatics isn't possible at the moment). In fact, that sounds fun - so stories about that would be much more interesting. I'll do some research into how difficult that task might be, and report back.

I guess I am feeling pressured to make my actual life more interesting because I still haven't come up with any solid ideas for a novel outside of this bizarre autobiography. It is not the usual format for that type of writing, but I'm not worried about fitting this into a specific genre or label. I'm just writing. I just want to get better at getting words out. Once I know how to use them better, I will be able to jumble them together in a way that tells stories more interesting than the ones I live - or at least I can live the stories through writing them instead of risking my job security by becoming increasingly more ridiculous as a means to create novel topics.

A more daring version of myself wouldn't be worried about risking my job security in the pursuit of an epic tale, as long as I wasn't hurting anyone. I'm fairly certain that all plausible potential versions of myself would not want to hurt anyone, although I don't know how plausible a courageous Andy might be. I guess that would bring in some much needed tension to drive a plot, but I don't actually want to cause harm to anyone in real life. I also don't want to imagine causing harm to anyone I know in real life, so I might just have to start creating characters that are not solely based on people I see in real life. I feel like I need to learn how to take attributes of completely random commuters and image a whole new person instead of actually imagining what that person's life is like. I'm not manipulating a real person's story, but that of a fictional character who happens to bare a resemblance to someone I once saw on the bus.

It is time to create a character and just get to know them, instead of only getting to know myself. The more I learn about myself, the less I feel like I know about the whole of myself - if that makes any sense. I'm not sure if I'm explaining it well. I open up a room, but feel like there are ten rooms leading off it that I don't yet have access to. I'm sure the character will even teach me more about myself (perhaps the character will strong arm a door or two for me) when I choose which way to lead him in whatever plot comes up. I think that I will just create a character, and see where they take me. If it is somewhere I don't want to go, I can always stop the story. It should be as easy as closing the door, or closing this document.

Doing aerobics behind people and trying to do it quietly is kind an unnerving rush when you are out of shape, like I am. I would get a couple steps into my antics before having to stop and pretend I was immersed in something else. I think I was successful, but you can never really tell if other people brushed the feeling off or just returned to ignoring you. When in doubt, I just pretend I've found some of Figaro's hair on my clothing and mime picking it off. So far, I think it has worked just fine.

Perhaps some day, I will graduate to using throwing stars or something more interesting than the hokey pokey. I would really have to work on my aim, not to mention they would leave evidence in walls that I had been messing around. It is fun to visualize, but not very practical.

***

Today is the day to stop hoping that I will get up the courage or genius or whatever it is I am waiting to arrive so I can move forward on this journey. I've decided to start my story, but I want to keep it within these pages as a way of documenting my process. I know that it is going to be rough, and I'll likely have to do several drafts before I am happy with what I'm writing, but for now I just want to play around with it and breathe life into some characters. I'll switch to Italics when I'm writing pieces of the story, which will also make it easier for me to find them and extract them when I do the editing process.

I'm really quite nervous. How does someone start? If someone cannot find a great opening, should they even bother to start in the first place? Should I skip the opening all together and get straight to whatever I can get out of my brain the fastest? That seems disingenuine - like starting to watch "Law & Order" if you missed the opening sequence. I can never do it. If I don't know what is going on with the case, or what the case even really is, I can't bring myself to watch the episode. I think that writing will be a little like that. Even though I don't really know where I will be going with it, I need to start it somewhere instead of jumping into the middle of things. I can always change it up later, but I need a beginning. With that in mind, here I go:

Within a small town, containing very little to classify it as extraordinary, there was a man named Randell who lived alone, and preferred it that way.

Not a brilliant start, but I shouldn't let that keep me from continuing, because sometimes when you are "in for a penny, [you need to be] in for a pound."

When he woke up in the morning, he was free to go about his morning ritual, not having to bother with wearing pants. He didn't bother combing his mop of shaggy brown hair unless he was about the leave the house, and he grew sick years ago of other people inflicted their opinions about his style upon him. He preferred his hair when it spontaneously created strange shapes upon his head. These shapes were of constant amusement to him as he'd wander around his house and caught glimpses of himself in reflections of windows, or while making toast. He rarely bothered to get it cut, but that had more to do with the logistics of not wanting to do it himself, not that he was a fan of paying very much for the service.

Although Randell preferred to live alone, the house had not always been his (as houses often have histories of different owners once they reach a certain age). The house had belonged to his parents, and passed on to him when they unexpectedly died in a car crash several years ago. Although he missed them, for they had been wonderful parents, the house held comfort for him. It also helped that they had recently paid off the mortgage before that farm truck swerved to miss a deer and hit his folks' Chrysler instead. He'd taken a leave of absence from work after his parents died, and never really went back full time after he received their life insurance and a settlement from the driver of the truck. He supposed that people in the town likely thought of him as a recluse or a hermit, since he was rarely seen in town. He preferred to run laps of the property and keep his muscles well-trained by lifting the heaviest things he could find around the yard. He didn't believe in going to a gym for vanity, but rather liked how it felt to sweat. He preferred the freedom and the silence in his home to the pity in the eyes of people who remembered who his parents had been. Randell hated feeling the pity of other people. Years later, he was still treated as though the wound was fresh. He had moved on. The town refused to do so.

I guess that serves as a decent introduction to this character. I'll have to flesh out a few more details, and figure out what his story from this point forward is. The good thing is that the story could be anything; the bad thing is that there are so many different paths I could choose to lead him down, and I think it might be difficult to decide which would be best. I might just have to roll a die or pick ideas out of a hat if none of them give me a gut instinct.

I need to remember that this isn't expected to be perfect by anyone else, so I shouldn't expect perfection either. I can always rewrite the story if it doesn't turn out well, right?

My feline companion has decided he desperately needs my attention, which must mean it is time to take a break so I can feed him.

* * *

The road into town was getting extremely full of potholes and obstacles due to neglect. Randell wasn't surprised. He was pretty sure not many other people used it since the Summer, when there was a lot of camping in secluded spots off the road that people seemed to think no one knew about. He didn't use it often enough to complain to the town to fix it. The others would be back in the Spring once things started to heat back up and they would started to complain. Complaining himself would, of course, mean he would have to talk to people about it, and he avoided making more contact than needed when he went into town. He briefly considered writing a letter about it, but decided it wasn't worth the time or hassle. He was sure someone else would realize how bad the road was getting if they used it, and would complain themselves. Driving the roller coaster once a month was enough of a fun challenge that he was not motivated to talk to anyone about improving the conditions. A myriad of different hues, reds, oranges, yellows and molding greens flurried over his truck as he slowly worked his way along the road. He was starting to speed up, as he was impatient to get in, get out, and go home.

"I might even just make it a personal project," Randell thought to himself. "I could use the fallen trees for firewood in the Winter anyway." He'd have to make an extra tip out on the road, since he wouldn't be able to fit all his supplies and the excess timber in one load of his pickup truck. "I'll decide later if I'm up for it." It didn't have to be done immediately, after all, but it would be better if he did it before it started to rain. Drying wood before being able to burn it effectively was a pain in the ass.

Some of the biggest holes were masked by blankets of Autumn leaves, but Randell navigated his way toward town without much delay. He always made a list, so he wouldn't have to spend any more time than necessary selecting his purchases. More time meant more people. More people meant more pity. If he spent too much time surrounded by their pity, he felt he might explode.

***

I've been thinking that I should add a female character, mostly because it will be interesting to write about one. I don't know if I am keen on writing a love story with Randell as the lead, but maybe he just needs a friend who doesn't take any pity on him. I actually think I would go a little crazy if I had been living like him for so long. I mean, I'm not huge on socializing, but I enjoy observing people too much to live in such extreme isolation. I guess my life is a little easier in that I don't feel any pity when I walk around – at worst, I feel completely invisible until I get in someone's way. The longest I can go completely alone is a couple of days, and then I just need to feel other people around me. Occasionally, it strikes my fancy to even chit chat with people. Randell needs, at least, someone to talk to (because I don't think his day to day is going to sustain the entirety of an interesting story unless it is shaken up a bit), so I'll have to figure out a reason for someone to come to his place - or someone for him to bump into when he goes into the town proper for supplies.

Maybe this woman is new to the town, and therefore doesn't have the same sense of sorrow for Randell that everyone else clings to. I think he would be very attracted to the idea of someone just treating him like a human being, rather than a hermit or a broken man. I'll sit with this idea for a while before I just toss someone else into the mix.

"Fuck," Randell muttered under his breath as he felt the truck start to sink on one corner. "Of course I have to get a fucking flat." Randell was fine with fixing his truck by himself, but all of his tools were at home. He knew he would have to rely on the mechanic in town, and that meant staying longer than he liked. He slung himself from the cabin of the truck and didn't even lock the door - no one would come by this stretch of road who would have an interest in his empty truck, anyway.

Randell wasn't in the mood to be thankful that he was only a couple minutes walking distance from the road that officially started the edge of town. Although a breakdown midway through his trail would have made his day longer, he would have at least had the option of going home to grab his own tools instead of getting the mechanic to give him a tow and fix his flat. He wouldn't even be able to load his shopping into the truck until it was fixed.

It took him about 45 minutes of walking, but he finally arrived at the one mechanic in town that he knew about, and it only took another 5 minutes to describe where his car was and give over this keys. The mechanic only made special mention of his name and told Randell that he was sorry about his folks once before moving onto the actual business at hand, a record.

"It is going to take a little while to fix the flat," the elderly man behind the plywood desk crooned. "And you're probably hungry, so why don't you wander over to the dinner and grab yourself a bite to eat, and I'll call on you there when it is done?" Randell figured it might be easier to hide from glances in a corner booth rather than sitting in front of the mechanic shop, so he agreed and started on the old man's directions that lead a couple of blocks away. He supposed other people might think it was a treat to have a stranger cook for them, but Randell had grown accustomed to just grazing whenever he felt like it, so sitting down to an intentional meal felt off to him. Perhaps he'd just have coffee to pass the time, if that didn't keep the waitress on his ass about refills.

***

The weather changed drastically over night and now I cannot seem to keep warm, no matter how many layers I pull on, or how much tea I brew. The flesh beneath my fingernails is nearly glowing a faint purple. I almost wish I had a wood burning fire place, like Randell, but any time I have ever lit so much as a candle it has freaked Figaro out. I have heard of cats hating water, but fire is a new one for me.

It would be lonely out in the middle of nowhere, which is where I picture Randell's home, but it would also be cozy. I've even turned my heat up in the apartment (and I must admit to having some jealousy over how smugly warm Figaro always appears to be) but something tells me the heating system is on the fritz again, because not much seems to be coming from the vents.

I detest being cold. Like the effect of chilling any other substance, it slows me down. I find it incredibly difficult to get out of bed in the morning, knowing the atmosphere outside of my blankets is vastly more frigid than that within my bed. Showering always seems like an impossible task when I think about it for too long, too. I always fear that there won't be adequate hot water, and there is nothing worse than a lukewarm or cold shower when all you are craving is the warmth of bed. If you shower cold, you are cold when you become dry, and no amount of socially acceptable layers can bring your body temperature back up. There seems to come a point where extra clothing is only effective in restricting movement rather than trapping escaping heat.

I would rather be too hot than be too cold. The only thing that happens when I get too hot is a tendency to nap, whereas falling asleep when I am cold is an endless nightmare. Even if I manage to drift off, it never feels as though I truly slept, and a new gust of chilled air attacks my body, bringing me back to consciousness.

I'm going to check the hot water supply. I have a feeling that the occupants of the whole building might be doing the same, so my hopes aren't high. If I could just submerge myself in hot water, and leave before it gets cold, I might return to feeling somewhat human, instead of a frozen ornament that could be plucked from my apartment by a giant and trapped within a snow globe for the rest of eternity. I can feel my brain function slowing, and if I get to the chattering teeth phase, I am going to have to find a superheated shopping mall to stand around in so I can become human temperature again. At least I would be able to people watch, which could be good research for this project. I'm sure Figaro wants his alone time. It's probably not the same, going about your cat duties when there is a human in the way.

I wasn't satisfied with my mostly warm shower, so I bundled up and went to sit in the food court of the nearest mall, sipping a hot chocolate in an attempt to warm me up from the inside as well as outside. Seriously, what is with the temperatures in shopping centres? It is as though they keep the food courts so warm because they either want to watch people nap or get them out and shopping again as quickly as possible. At least they don't use cold air, I suppose, although I am sure that would drive up food sales during the summer months.

I noticed a blonde woman a few tables away that I believe can inspire an interesting addition to the novel. Instead of describing the actual woman, I'll incorporate some of her features into this new character description that I have been mulling over in my head.

The only reason she found herself serving several pots of coffee per day, the aroma of which she found disgusting, was she hated the last small town she lived in more than she hated serving coffee. She pushed her gentle blonde curls out of her eye with the back of her hand and lifted another full pot with the ease of someone who knew all too well the labours of working in a diner. A glimmer of sweat ran down the bridge of her slightly crooked nose and dived onto the sleeve of her greasy diner shirt. She made a note to run a load of laundry as soon as she got off shift.

"At least the staff here is friendly," Cynthia thought to herself, trying to push memories of her past out of her mind. She'd hated the drudgery her old life had become - she always pulled double shifts because other people couldn't make it in, and her paycheque never seemed to be worth the hours she spent being stalked by her boss. Although she had had a sweet customer now and then, they were few and far between, and no one ever tipped her when she went above and beyond to serve them quickly. It also didn't help that her boss kept hitting on her.

"I won't have that problem here," she smiled to herself. The owner of this new cafe was not only a married man, but so was his husband. She was glad to live in a town where that wasn't a big deal to any of the customers. She assumed it was because the town was at least three towns from a church, and from her experience, the further away from blind prejudice, the less judgmental and more accepting the people. She'd noticed this trend while hitch-hiking between different small towns in her youth; she'd never be a city girl, but she grew bored of small places if there was not a hook to keep her there.

The hook in the last rat trap of a town could be described as a rat himself, but she figured that he wouldn't bother to look for her, no matter how jealous he pretended to be of her long hours at work. She had known he had other girls on the side for quite some time, and she had even been completely fine with that once she realized she didn't love him. She just hated that he lied about it, and expected her to always be around, doing whatever he wanted of her, while he was out doing whatever he wanted. She wasn't his property. No one owned her, and no one ever would.

She didn't take many things with her when she escaped the last town; she was used to travelling light. She always seemed able to find a room to rent that was at least partly furnished in whatever town she visited, and when she was really lucky, she didn't have to share a bathroom or a kitchen. In this town she just had a room, but only one other person lived in the house: an elderly widow named Dorothy who just seemed happy to have someone to cook for. After a full day at the diner, Cynthia wasn't usually all that hungry, but was grateful to not have to prepare food for herself. The old lady usually turned in pretty early, so she wasn't forced to chit chat longer than was comfortable. Cynthia had only been there a couple of weeks, but she was growing fond of Dorothy, despite her tendency to try to not get attached to people. Either she'd leave or the old lady would die one day, and she didn't want to broken up about it whenever one of those two things came first. She'd left behind so many faces and names in so many towns that she wasn't always able to recall them all with clarity, and that made it easier to move on.

"Can I get the bill when you have a chance, Cynthia?" one of the regulars asked over the edge of his paper. She filled his cup anyway, knowing that he'd be around long enough to drink it, and also knowing that he was extremely patient about getting the paperwork done. She tore his slip out of her notepad immediately anyway, muffling the noise in her apron so she could leave it without disturbing him. It had become their pattern, and he seemed to like it that way. She saw an increase in her tips as soon as she started "being sneaky," even though she assumed they both knew she was doing it each time. She was game to play along when it directly increased the tip he left on the same sandwich and cup of coffee each day.

Without being asked, she refilled the decaf cup of the table in the corner, doing her best impression of an invisible person, because they never liked being interrupted. It never took her long to pick up on the customer patterns in a new town, because each town had its own version of the same type of customers. She'd worked diners in more towns than the number of her age, so she knew the habits better than she remembered faces or names. The habits stayed the same, but the faces and names changed.

The bell on the door clanged and she couldn't help but turn to see which of her regulars was arriving - just in time for a fresh pot of coffee - but this guy was new to her. She had a way with the faces that belonged in each of the towns that she had worked and lived in over her life, but this face didn't fit, as though he was a piece from a puzzle she had yet to start.

Randell slunk into a cramped, semi private booth and kept his head down. The place was a little busy for his taste, but he figured he might still go unnoticed if he just kept quiet.

"Coffee?" Cynthia crooned, sliding up to Randell's booth. He was almost certain that he hadn't seen this woman before. Maybe she just looked different from years ago, since he didn't pay much attention to the town folk, but she seemed about his age and he felt he would have remembered a woman with her striking features. His conclusion was she might not be from this town, although how she ended up here was a complete mystery to him. If he were more comfortable anywhere else, that's where he would be.

"Yeah, sure," he replied, turning over the cup that was preset on the table. She slid a menu onto his table as the coffee jumped from the pot to his cup, but she didn't immediately leave, like most waitresses tend to do. She lingered for a second, and Randell started to rethink the possibility that she knew who he was.

"Are you from around here?" she finally asked. She quickly added, "It's just that even though I'm relatively new, I don't forget faces and I haven't seen you around."

Randell raised the cup to his lips, cooling his beverage with an exhale. "I live on the outskirts of town; I don't come in much," he replied, his eyes darting between the window and her blonde curls. He wasn't completely sure, as it can be hard to tell with people who work for tips, but she might be coming onto him. He would be lying if he said he didn't find her attractive, but he wasn't wanting to draw too much attention to himself. If he did, someone would probably tell the pretty girl his sob story, and she'd adopt the glimmer of pity he'd just witnessed in the old mechanic's eyes.

"That would explain it," she replied, resting the bottom edge of the coffee pot against his table. "I knew that we hadn't met before. I'm Cynthia." She made a small wave of her fingers with the unoccupied hand. "Let me know if you want anything to eat."

Randell hadn't even begun to form a reply when he realized she was half way across the diner. She glanced back at him, just for a moment, but it was long enough for Randell to see something he hadn't seen in this town for a very long time - eyes that just wanted to look at him, and not weep for him. There was something about this girl that drew him in with her every move. He decided that maybe he was hungry after all.

***

Sometimes I wonder if there is anyone out there who observes me. It doesn't have to be on a regular basis, like I do with certain people with whom I often cross paths. You read stories where the main character has "the usual" waiting for them at their favourite restaurant or bar or coffee shop, but that has never happened to me, no matter how many times I go into my local cafe before work. It isn't as though I have a complicated order. I just drink black coffee (and unlike my newest character, I find the aroma charming), but the employees always have to ask, as though my face doesn't even show up on their radar. Maybe they just need to drink more of their own product to keep alert, and I'm just being sensitive because the guy in the brown over coat gets the same order so many times when I am in there that even I know what he drinks (large half caf extra foam latte). What ever happened to just black coffee being a staple? Even adding cream or sugar makes sense to me, although I had to cut down both for health reasons a couple of years ago and eventually just became used to coffee without embellishment.

In some ways I am fine with my anonymity, because I get flustered when too much attention is tossed my way. When I become a focal point, I feel as though I am expected to keep this incredible beach ball of energy afloat above the surrounding crowd of people and pretty much always feel like I am that loser who drops the ball and loses the game for the entire group. On the other hand, I get lonely like everyone else. I saw a comic once that depicted a guy as though he were a cat: When he was at home, he wanted to go out; when he was out, he wanted to go home. It rang very true with how I feel sometimes, and not just because my closest companion actually is a cat. I never want to be the life of the party, but it would be nice to be invited every once in a while, so to speak (minus all the office parties).

If I were a character in the story I am writing, I would likely be a patron at the diner who sits by himself, rarely has his cup refilled because he is forgotten by the waitress (or waiter) unless the table next to him is occupied, noticed only due to his proximity to others. The fictional character in this diner who represents me would always calculate his bill and tip in his head before the waitress comes around to settle up, and leave the cash on the table without causing any stir. Since she hadn't actually delivered the cheque by the time my character had left, the waitress would momentarily think that it was odd that the money was on the table with the bill was in her apron, but she wouldn't dwell on it (after all, I tend to be a nice tipper because waitresses and waiters do a job for which I would never have the courage). For all she knows, a ghost had the egg salad sandwich and cup of black coffee, but as long as that ghost paid his tab and tipped well, she wouldn't mind the mystery.

Maybe this is why both the characters I have written into focal points of this story are loners - because I wouldn't know how to write an extrovert and do them justice. I could write the caricature of an extrovert, full of clichés about them talking too much or too loudly, but I am much better at being in the head of a man who spends most of his time alone, and a woman who - well, hides from her problems by moving on to the next situation and leaving the old one behind. I do that. I bury problems, like not being able to express my creativity, and move on to the next place where I can find a paycheque. It doesn't matter that I have been at the same firm for twelve years now - I always bury myself in work at the office when I am avoiding a personal problem. I guess I have been writing some of what I know, after all.

***

"This town doesn't seem any worse than any of the others I've been in," Cynthia mused, slipping onto the stool next to him at the bar. Randell had long since finished his sandwich, paid his tab and moved to the diner bar to give up his table, but the mechanic hadn't called him yet. Although under usual circumstances he'd be annoyed, Randell didn't really mind right now.

Cynthia was off work, but not rushing to leave and put on that load of laundry she had promised herself. "So what did it do to you to make you so flinchy?" she asked, leaning on the bar with one elbow and turning her eyes fully to his. Those clear eyes beckoned to his, with no trace of pity. He didn't want to put it there.

"It is both the most simplistic thing and the most difficult thing in the world to explain right now," Randell started. He didn't want to lie, but he didn't need her to join the legion of town folk who looked at him "that way."

"I've got time," Cynthia said, rooting herself firmly to the stool; he wanted to trust her, and she seemed to really want to know.

"The thing is, most people around here treat me a little differently," he continued. "They don't do it on purpose - at least I sure hope they don't, because it is a mighty long time to keep up an act. I just don't want to tell you the cause and have you adopt that same way of treating me."

"Short of you murdering someone, I think I can handle it," Cynthia chuckled, "and even then, you probably had your reasons." She didn't think her joke had been on target, but you never know.

"Well, this story has death, but it wasn't me who did it," Randell replied. "My folks. Car crash. When I was young enough that the town still thought I was just a kid. Now I can't go anywhere without any of the old timers thinking not a day has passed and that I must still be completely broken up."

"I'm sorry to hear that." She sounded genuine, but Randell avoided her eyes. If they were going to change, he wanted to hold onto the pleasant memory a little longer.

"It was tough, but it was a long time ago, and I have moved on, unlike this town." He decided it was time to check. If there was a glimmer of pity, he would rather walk home than continue to seemingly pour his soul out to a stranger. His eyes flicked up to hers, then away, and back again. She blinked. Her crystal eyes were just as clear as when he first noticed them.

"So," Cynthia shifted her weight to bring herself closer to his stool. "What do you do for fun around here?"

I wonder if Randell is so lonely that he would jump at the chance to be with someone, simply because she didn't have any of the usual traits he detests in the people who live near him. I'm pretty sure that I would be wanting some quality company after basically a decade alone. As much as Figaro has been around for me, there is only so much you can count on when it comes to companionship from your cat. I'm not judging - that's just the way Figaro is. For the matter of Randell's solitude and whether or not is should be broken, Cynthia gets a say in all of this now, and I wonder if she is attracted to this loner. It's not as though I am judging him either, but sometimes people don't look past one label or another to notice that someone is a whole person, not one attribute. Finance Guy is a pretty big wall for people to try to climb, so I can expect Loner Guy to have similar boundaries.

I don't feel qualified to make these decisions; I guess any author just has to guess how his characters would react based on what little he knows of them. I kind of feel like I have scooped a couple people out of the ether, put them in a box and now I am just waiting to see what they do.

***

The sex was incredible.

I actually cannot really believe that I am attempting to write a sex scene (didn't I originally say something about not wanting Randell to be a romantic lead?), but it seems to make perfect sense with these characters and the way they are behaving. Another piece of advice I heard once was that the next logical action was probably the right one to go with, but I'm definitely not writing what I know, as I've never had sex that I would describe as incredible, and even the pornography I've watched hasn't seemed like it would be incredible. Most of it seems incredibly improbable and awkward. It is just a word that I have heard bandied about when other people have talked about their own experiences - both in real life and characters on television. I feel like these characters deserve it (they are both very lonely in their own ways), and I'll try to do it service, even if it is not my specialty.

It all started with a lock of their eyes. In that moment, they both knew that they wanted each other, and they wanted each other right that moment. Their attraction drew them close together, a python wrapping them both and starting to squeeze. She tilted her head up to meet his lips, and shut herself off to the world outside of this moment.

It wasn't as though Randell had been celibate since his parents died, but his trips to the cities where he found some anonymity, and partners that didn't try to baby him because of his past, were few and far between. Once he had picked a girl up off street corner after a long night at the bar, since her company came at a reasonable rate, but their encounter had not truly satisfied him.

Cynthia was hungry for Randell's body, and a connection to someone who wasn't her bastard ex. She'd never been one to jump right into bed, but her attraction to him was magnetic, and she didn't even consider denying herself the pleasure of pressing against his well-muscled body.

Their hands wandered, mapping out each other's torsos; the rhythm was soft at first, but the pressure of their fingers grew harder as their hands wandered lower. He grasped her hips and pulled her toward him, knowing she could feel him through his jeans.

I don't know how much description I should get into before I'll be classified as a complete pervert. Do sex scenes between two characters who seem like they are hitting it off qualify someone for the title of a pervert? I kind of feel like I am looking at them through a window or something, and that is not very comfortable. It is one thing to watch porn - because the "performers" know that someone (or lots of someones) is going to see them, but spying on characters I created like this has an odd feeling attached to it. I feel like I've built up a sense of passion, although there is a lot of exposition, but I don't really know where to go from there. Maybe I'll just leave them hanging for a while, and come back to this scene later if my awkwardness dissipates. He's certainly waited a long time, so I know he can hold out a little longer.

Am I really discussing how I am actively cockblocking a fictional character? I didn't know that was part of a writer's process.

* * *

I accidentally made eye contact with Gabriella today.

It must have to do with me being a little tired and, because of that, my reaction time to her turning my way was delayed, which caused this whole situation to unfold. I'm tired, because I was up late thinking about my story, but was unable to actually put anything down on the page. I'm very indecisive about where to go with all of this. I kept asking Figaro his opinion, but he ignored me. Typical selfish cat, never there for me when I really need him.

I'm usually always so careful. It often feels like I am invisible when I people watch - as though I can take in every physical detail of a person without them noticing, as though I don't exist, or don't exist in the same dimension in which they are running around.

Her eyes are brown. Very deep brown. I could tell from across the lobby, and even though I had noticed the colour before, I had never fully looked into her eyes until that moment. I rarely look anyone fully in the eye, but I guess that is what happens when someone catches you looking at them.

I think we were both a little startled, to be honest. There was a jolt that went through her shoulders that mirrored the jolt through my own. The stunned look that blanketed her face when my eyes pulled away slowly morphed into a soft smile when I glanced back to see if she could still see me. I hadn't regained my invisibility. I don't know if that superpower will ever be as strong again; a sliver of kryptonite is hidden near me now.

She could still see me. I know this for a definite fact. We caught each others' eyes again, but this time it was significantly longer before one of us looked away, as though we were on an unspoken dare. This time she broke the glance, but quickly hopped her eyes back to mine and a blush of deep red rose to her cheeks. I felt an alien smile creep across my face before I became aware of how completely flustered I felt throughout my entire body. I packed up the remnants of my lunch and scurried toward the elevator, unable to cast even a single glance in her direction. My toe tapped against the cool, smooth tile as I waiting for the doors to slide apart. I pushed the button again. I know that it doesn't make the elevator come any faster, but it gives me something to do with my hands, and even a second of distraction from feeling completely vulnerable is a huge relief.

"You work up on 14th, right?" I heard a voice to my right. Even though I'd never heard words from her mouth before, I knew who was talking to me. No one really ever spoken to me in the lobby, except the cashier or barista at the coffee cart, so the list of potential conversationalists was very short.

Gabriella had never been so close to me before. I was relatively sure we had never taken the same elevator, as that would be the only time I could foresee us being so close and I would have noticed her in my close space if she had been there in the past. Her eyes were even deeper in close proximity. I almost forgot to respond, because my mind was going on about the calculations of her proximity to me.

"Yeah, that's where I spend 40 hours a week, " I blurted. The elevator doors finally parted, and we stepped inside, dangerously close to bumping shoulders. No one else needed to use the elevator at that point, it seemed, and we were completely alone as the doors slid shut. I was still in a robotic state of shock, and beating myself up for not having something better to say in response to her simple question. I could have introduced myself. I could have asked what tipped her off. I could have said anything that didn't make me seem like a workaholic, but these ideas came later, when the moment was gone.

"I'm just on top of you," Gabriella replied, nearly immediately adding, "That didn't sound quite right. I'm on the 15th." She pressed the buttons for each of our floors and stepped back to stand beside me.

"What do you do?" I stuttered, genuinely curious, as I had never bothered to figure out which company occupied the floor above my own. I secretly thought it sounded more like I was just trying to be polite, and hoped that it didn't sound routine outside of my head.

"I work in fashion," she replied, and her tone made it sound as though she likely assuming I wasn't actually interested in her life story. Damn. This woman I've been observing for months talks to me, but of course I come off as being completely uninterested. Typical. If I had known we would eventually talk, I would have come up with something thrilling to talk about.

"And what do you do in fashion?" The light indicating the passing floors was drawing dangerously close to the mid-teens, and I didn't want this conversation to end. She glanced over at me. She must have seen honest curiosity in my face (how she saw it through my sweat of panic, I'll never know), which is likely what caused her to pause.

"I am in charge of fabric acquisition," she admitted. Smoothing on a velvety layer of sarcasm, she continued. "I'm sure that sounds thrilling."

"Hey, you are talking to a Finance Guy, so everything is more thrilling than what I do," I blurted. "I'm Andy, by the way." Before I could stop myself, I extended my hand, like this was a business meeting. I was even more horrified when I realized the palm of my hand was probably really sweaty.

"Gabriella," she replied. It took everything in my being to not reply with, "I know." That would have come off rather creepy, I imagine. Fortunately, she stopped me from tossing my stalker reply in there by actually shaking my hand. Her hand was warm and soft, likely heated by the remnants of the coffee in the cup she shifted to take my hand. I hoped it didn't squeeze too hard or long, and that she didn't notice the uncomfortable moisture level.

The chime dinged and the door slid open. My stop. I lifted my grasp from her hand, but it didn't retract at a speed that made me think I'd been keeping her hand encased in mine too long.

"I should get back to those numbers," I mumbled, nearly tripping over my own feet on the way through the void left by the shiny doors. I turned around awkwardly and briefly pictured this as the the door to a house, as though we were on a first date and this was the moment where a brave man goes for the good night kiss.

"I'll see you again, I'm sure," Gabriella replied as the doors started to slink shut. No goodnight kiss, I guess, but I wouldn't hold that against her, considering it was about that moment when reality kicked back in and I could suddenly hear all the people talking on their phones, and the *glug glug* of the water fountain next to the elevator made its way into my range of hearing. I didn't realize how silent everything had seemed while Gabriella was next to me. My floor now felt like a mad house, as our mutual stillness burst into frantic antics of people from all departments going about their loosely choreographed dance. The sound wall that hit me was that of an orchestra warming up, and playing dischords at their highest volume.

I quickly slunk to my desk and sat down, hoping that I would fit back into the action seamlessly, and that I would be left to my own devices for the rest of the day. The fantastic thing about being the guy who deals with things that no one really understands is that if I just hunch over my desk, and occasionally mutter, people assume I am very busy. They reflect on the problems that they have when working with numbers, and leave me alone because they conclude that they couldn't possibly be of help. I work rather quickly, and spend a lot of time polishing my Solitaire score. I even perfected the art of exactly how to tilt my monitor so that no one can see it unless they come an alarming distance into my space, which a) doesn't happen often and b) gives me time to close the game before they pore over my shoulder at things they generally don't understand anyway. I can fool most people with a desktop backdrop that looks like an Excel document, because no one stops to study what I have on my screen.

I spent those last few work hours taking way too long to finish my games of Solitaire (not even hitting in my top ten score bracket) because my mind kept wandering to Gabriella. She was not just this person I saw from a distance every once in a while anymore. She had actually talked to me, and I proved she was real (not some character I had fabricated in my head) by shaking her hand. Would this get me off my butt to maybe seeing if I could have more conversations, and specifically conversations with her? I know this was wasn't exactly a legendary moment in the history of first conversations, but it was a start. Could she, some day, be attracted to me? I had kind of given up on the concept of any pretty woman being attracted to me a long time ago. Do I dare to hope that I was wrong?

By the time I got up to leave the office, I felt like I was getting ahead of myself. A part of me was hoping she'd be in the elevator, exactly as I had left her a few hours before, and that we could do our trip in reverse, just so I could take it as a sign to try to ask her on a date. Do people even do that anymore - ask other people on official dates? How does one even go about doing that? When I was a teenager, you always asked someone if they wanted to hang out, and the romantic nature of the meeting was implied. I don't think that is the way it goes when you are an adult; why does the language of creating a personal event have to change as we get older? Maybe it hasn't and I should just imply a date by asking to hang out?

I'm out of practice. In truth, I don't even know if I was ever really in practice, so I don't know if that phrase applies to me. All I do know is this is what it feels like to be nervous in a very excited way, and I haven't felt this in a very long time.

I've only just realized that I came in through my front door and sat right at my laptop to record this story. I didn't stop to contemplate dinner - it didn't even register in my mind or body that I am hungry, although I really should eat. Figaro has been running around my feet like a possessed kitten, but I've hardly given him a glance or a tiny reassurance that he'll be fed soon. I had to record this meeting, even if it turns out to be the only time we actually talk to each other. Knowing me, this high will fade and the next time I see her, I will go back to carefully turning my head when I can sense that she will be looking in my general direction soon.

Although, wouldn't it be fantastic if she decided to talk to me first? That would give me the confidence I need to keep a conversation going, and at least figure out if she is available. I didn't notice a ring, but that means very little in this day and age of boyfriends, complicated relationships and so on - not to mention I shook her right hand, not her left, so that is the one on which I was focused, and a wedding ring is traditionally on the left hand.

I'm thinking way too much about this. The whole ordeal couldn't have lasted more than five minutes between her catching me looking at her and her saying that maybe we'd see each other again. It would be nice if it turns out that she won't just look right through me when we are in the lobby at the same time. People from work do that, but that is the way I prefer to keep it with most of them. It would be nice to have someone with whom I care share a genuine smile. I guess that makes me seem more lonely than I am on a day to day basis, but if I could choose, I would want someone who understands me to share my time. I am obviously capable of being alone, but sometimes it is nice to think that there could be someone out there who would brighten my day, and want me to be in their day. I would like to have someone to challenge me. If I had a partner in my life, I might have started this project sooner, because having someone around who understands you and can look into what you are doing with your time gives a whole new perspective on what challenges you are sulking away from that you should really at least attempt.

Randell picked her up with one arm and pressed her against the kitchen counter, never taking his lips from her face. "How do you feel about losing some of this unnecessary fabric?" he murmured between kisses, his fingers raking her back as hers tugged at his hair.

"I agree that it is unnecessary," she moaned, eager to see with her eyes what her fingers were already feeling.

I am going to be honest here - this is what I would want to happen between Gabriella and I after a few dates (there is that word again: dates) and getting to know each other better (this term or phrase is something with which I am a lot more comfortable). This would be how I would want things to be, meaning I would have to gain some confidence first. I would also have to gain some rock hard abs, but those are less important to my fantasy scenario with Gabriella. I would be content with her wanting to acquisition the fabric right off my body.

It almost doesn't seem right to watch Randell and Cynthia through the whole process. Maybe I'll just gloss over a few details. I can always fill them in later if I feel the need. It almost feels like I am cheating on them by thinking about a different woman while writing their sex scene.

The sun had gone down outside his secluded cabin by the time they each lay back, coated in a slick sweat and gasping for breath.

"That was quite a workout," Cynthia whispered, her breasts heaving and her lungs trying to return to a normal rate of movement.

"I always thought I was pretty physically fit," Randell replied, rolling to cup her face and bring her eyes to his. "But you gave me a run for my money."

They were both fast asleep within moments, neither realizing that either had slipped off to a place of rest and post-satisfaction bliss.

I no longer feel like a stalker, looking through the window, but more like a theatre-goer watching from the safety of a cinema screen. The devil may be in the details, so I am content with keeping him behind the walls of Randell's cabin. He might come in handy later, but for now, I, like my characters, must rest.

I woke up this morning with almost no motivation to write. I don't know what should come next. Should I reveal their "morning after" to the world? How do each of them feel about their night together? Will they want to do it again?

Do it. Huh. I sound like a teenager. Maybe one of them should just suggest that they should hang out again soon. I'm glad that teenage me isn't writing this, as I didn't think the awkwardness level could get much higher, but that would certainly do it.

Huh. There I go again.

"You don't have to risk another flat. I'm sure I can walk, and it won't take too long," Cynthia protested as the tempo-driven rocking of Randell's truck on the damaged road suddenly caused her stomach to flip. Why hadn't she noticed it was this rocky on the way to his cabin?

"It takes much longer to walk than you'd think," he replied, swerving to not hit a big hole and dipping into a little one instead. *"Besides, I have my tools this time, so I won't have to rely on that mechanic if another nail is waiting to ruin my day."*

"I seem to remember that mechanic being the reason I got to know you a little better," Cynthia replied, trying to flirt, partly as an attempt to mask her nauseated feeling. She hated bumpy roads, and must have been extremely distracted when they rode to his place the night before, because she didn't remember her stomach doing acrobatics the previous night. At least, she couldn't recall unpleasant acrobatics from last night.

"You have a point, but all the same, I'd rather not give him more money for a job I can do myself." Randell found a familiar rut in the road that he knew would take him on a safe path for a little while.

"That sounds like it might be your motto."

"I like to be self sufficient." He glanced over at her, and noticed she was turning a little green. "Are you okay?"

"I'll be fine. The bumps have subsided," she assured him. With perfect timing, the truck jerked to the right and bounced back into the groove Randell liked to ride.

"It shouldn't take too much longer," he replied, speeding up in an attempt to make the roller coaster end sooner.

~ ~ ~

"I won't be long, if you still want to take me up on that free lunch," Cynthia tossed the words over her shoulder as she dodged toward her front door. She needed to shower and change before her next shift. "You don't have to wait in your truck, either."

Randell was amused at her enthusiasm for no longer being in his truck, and equally grateful that she hadn't heaved all over it. He swung his weight from the driver seat and pocketed his keys, while slamming the door, as it always had problems shutting completely. He wasn't much for chit chat, and secretly hoped the old lady wasn't home.

~ ~ ~

They made a routine of getting together about once a week, when she had her scheduled days off. He would drive into town, pick up supplies, if he needed them, while she was finishing her shift, and then they would escape back to his place. Sometimes she stopped at home to grab a night bag, but usually she remembered to bring it with her to work. Neither wanted to admit it, but these trysts were the highlights of each of their weeks.

They were too absorbed in the mission of escaping the town and getting back to Randell's cabin to notice that there was a vehicle that often parked just outside her work, and occasionally followed them out of town. The driver took his time, and never followed directly down the road to Randell's. He knew exactly *where they were going, and didn't want to alert them. He was content in reading the local paper inside his car for a half hour - more like pretending to read it - before taking the bumpy road out of town. He'd park far enough away that they never heard his car on the road, and walk the rest of the way through the bush. The cabin windows never had the shades drawn, because Randell was used to being alone in the woods.*

Michael watched them grow passionate, undress each other and have sex through the windows on three separate occasions before he decided that they had to die.

***

I feel like this story is growing uncomfortable. I didn't plan in out ahead of time, and I am not longer trying to make it perfect (I knew from the beginning that perfection was not an attainable goal), but the path that they keep wanting to take me, at least in my mind, seems pretty dark. Is it right or even acceptable to feel fear of your own story? I don't know if I should fight the genre that this piece seems to want to embody or just keep following the natural course of events.

Work has grown hectic, and although I know that isn't the best excuse for not writing regularly, it is the one I am clinging to at the moment. I've had a couple of new projects dumped on my desk - mostly mindless data combing - but they are very time consuming and draining. By the time I get home, I just want to watch my crime dramas and fall asleep early, and that doesn't even take into consideration the quality time I've been spending with Figaro, because his little furry body warms me right up as long as he doesn't run away in the fickle way cats do after they are fed. You would think that they would feed, get sleepy and have no problem napping in your lap, but this guy seems to gain buckets of energy and use all of it in avoiding my cuddly advances. It's a good thing that I don't have a deadline for this story, because Randell and Cynthia are going to have to wait until I can give them a better quality of focus.

***

I saw Gabriella again today. I see her nearly every day, but I guess the important part of opening this story is that she saw me, too. In fact, she saw me first.

"Hi," she said, taking me by surprise. She had walked up behind me from the very tiny blind spot that exists from my usual vantage point of the lobby. I am not very proud to admit that I had to stifle a small shriek - but I am proud that it was stifled, nonetheless.

"Hey," I replied, covering the attempted shriek. I think she noticed, because a smile spread across her deep red lips. I momentarily compared them to wine in my head while they distracted me from her eyes. I panned my mind for something conversational. "Taking your last lunch break of the work week?"

"Yeah, I just have to get out of the office sometimes," she answered, placing her long legs (and the rest of her) in the seat next to me. "Do you mind if I join you?" I briefly wondered if the question was an after thought, considering she was already seated.

"Be my guest." She visibly slunk deeper into the cushions at my approval of her company. I would have been heartbroken if she had stood up and left instead of settling in. "I have been trying to remember to get out of the office when I can."

"You don't need those numbers bouncing around your brain all the time." She pulled a pasta salad from her purse and unlatched the glass lid. I automatically felt lazy for not bringing my own, homemade lunch and just eating from the food stand in the lobby.

"I imagine that you might go cross-eyed from looking at too many fabric patterns and textures just the same as I begin to jumble numbers after looking at them too long." I liked being able to bring a common denominator to our discussion by comparing the potential tediums of our work. I liked numbers just fine, but had a feeling that she enjoyed the fabric aspect of her work much more

52

than I enjoyed numbers. I momentarily mourned not having a more creative job.

"That has been known to happen," she admitted through a fork full of pasta salad, masked by a slender-fingered hand. "But I just thank the universe for having a job that I really like - for the most part." She finished chewing, swallowed, and continued speaking faster than I could interject. "There are some parts of the actual job that I don't enjoy, but I love that I get to tap into my creative brain. I wouldn't be able to go to work every day and do something tedious without rebelling in some way."

"It is easier than you think to mask creativity if you are pressured to do so," I blurted out before I even realize I had started to speak.

"Are you speaking from personal experience?" Her comment seemed to be a little off-handed, as though she wasn't actually curious but just making conversation. Maybe she bought into the same hooey I used to about how it wasn't possible to exist as a creative in a non-creative job.

"I never wanted to go into finance," I started, trying hard to keep my tone casual, even slightly subdued. If she actually didn't want to talk about my career path and how I was meant for something else, I didn't want to drag her into it. I was secretly bursting to share everything with her, though, because it would give us some common ground.

"Then why did you?" she asked. I could hear an edge of curiosity creep into her voice, even through the pasta salad and her elegant, mouth-masking hand.

"My folks," I admitted, suddenly feeling as though it wasn't a good enough answer. "It scared them when I did creative things, as though you cannot be successful and creative at the same time."

"I know how you feel. It is a tough gig to have both," Gabriella tucked her glass dish away after securing the lid. "There is a lot of competition and sometimes you really have to fight for what you want."

"I guess that is my problem," I replied. "I didn't fight. I didn't want to worry my folks. I just let it go."

"What did you leave behind that you wish you could revisit?" My admiration for her eagerness to chat about artistic endeavors filled my chest with the anticipation of sharing stories.

"I always wanted to be a writer."

"When is the last time you wrote something?" Her gaze met mine, and held it. I could feel her honest curiosity. How did I come to engage the full attention of this beautiful woman?

"I recently started a project." Little did she know that she was featured, let alone that I would record this conversation later. This transcript of our time together seems vastly more important than continuing the story aspect of this writing journal.

"Is there intrigue, daring plot twists, and a character that the audience will want to see succeed?" I couldn't tell if she was mocking creative writing light-heartedly or honestly hoping that was the synopsis of my project.

"Well, now that you mention it, my project doesn't seem all that exciting," I mumbled, purposefully laying on the self-deprecation a little thicker than my natural state. Usually it comes as part of the regular Andy package, but this time I played it like a card.

I gained a laugh, and what would have usually not been a bluff was met with a deliberate pat on my arm. Did I actually tickle her funny bone? "I'm sure that it is exciting."

"The most exciting part is that I am making myself do it," I confessed. "Perhaps the next tale will have more intrigue."

"Well, unless it is already over, there is always time to add intrigue. Even then, there is always the editing process." She paused, momentarily seeming to be lost in thought. "Whatever it is, I wish you well with it." She started to clear her things back into her purse. I didn't want her to leave so quickly.

"If you don't have plans already," I started, spewing the first words that came to mind that might cause her to pause and stay with me a little longer.

"What was that?" She asked, her head popping back up from the focus of reorganizing the items in her bag.

"I was wondering if you had plans this weekend," I stammered. The height of my current weekend plans considered of making sure that Figaro got the flea drops that his vet prescribed as a prevention method. Part of me thinks they were a money grab, but the other part of me really doesn't want to ever have to deal with fleas.

"Yeah, I'm having to travel out of town for a friend's wedding." She pushed a lock of hair out of her eyes. "More like a friend of a friend, since Anna didn't want to go alone."

"Oh, well, I'm sure you'll have fun anyway," I sputtered, desperate to change the subject before she realized that I had fumbled an attempt to ask her out.

"I'll tell you about it over coffee on Monday, if you like." That knowing smile was back on her lips. "Say, back here, around noon?" Her eyes found mine, and I could only nod to accept her invitation. "See you Monday, Andy."

I honestly cannot remember if I was able to choke out a "goodbye" as I watched her saunter toward the elevator. I felt frozen in place, as though this moment held the utmost importance. She was no longer someone I just saw on occasion. At very least, we were acquaintances, or friends, even; with a little encouragement, we might become more than that.

***

I arrived early on Monday to ensure I was seated at the exact same table where I last saw Gabriella on Friday. I had brought my own lunch, but I still purchased a tea from the food cart, mostly so I would have something to grasp that would keep my hands from shaking. Heavy ceramic mugs that are placed on the table in front of you are a haven for hands that you want to keep from shaking. I had tried to keep our meeting out of my mind all weekend, but it was hard to distract myself. The one hour that I don't think it came into my mind was while I was trying to wrestle Figaro into letting me apply the flea drops, but that was a huge ordeal consisting of hissing (on both our parts), attempts at scratching, and him being mad at me for the rest of the day. He only started to forgive me when I gave him some of the wet food that he likes instead of sticking to his usual diet of dry food. I didn't even get any writing done, which is unfortunate, because I assumed it would be the perfect distraction, but nothing came to me while I stared at the blank page, mocked by a blinking cursor.

By five minutes to noon, I had already told myself that I was now banned from looking at my watch, has the average change in time from one look to the next was about 20 seconds, and in one very special "fish memory" moment, the change was approximately 10 seconds. Looking at my watch wasn't going to make her appear any faster. For all I knew, she wasn't coming. Maybe she forgotten about our meeting, or her work meetings were running longer than anticipated. Maybe there wasn't anything interesting to talk about from the wedding of a friend of a friend, and she didn't want to waste time talking about a boring event with someone who lived in a different realm than she did.

"Hi," I heard from behind me. I was shaking from the two coffees I'd had this morning, and the few sips I had taken from the tea I was currently grasping, so I couldn't mask my slight jump. She let a giggle slip as she drop into the chair next to me.

"How do you keep sneaking up on me?" I asked, trying to sound light hearted, as though my heart wasn't trying to break out of my chest. I briefly wondered if she could see it trying to escape, as though this were a cartoon and such antics wouldn't result in severe physical damage.

"There is a semi-secret stairway," she pointed behind me to a door of which I had never taken much notice. "It is closer to my office than the main elevator, so when I want to sneak out, or want to sneak up, I use it."

"You feel a need to sneak around?" I teased, just trying to keep the conversation afloat with whatever cues I could find in her speech. I realized afterward that it could be taken very badly. An apologetic blush smeared itself across my face and my stomach lurched.

"Well, that always brings a little mystery into life, doesn't it?" she shot back, her voice playful. I breathed a sigh of relief to myself that she wasn't insulted, but her mention of mystery made me nervous. I don't know why - it is not as though mystery is a precursor to some foreboding event. I attribute it to a lack of courage in myself to be any form of intriguing, which would be the positive association of mystery. Sometimes I feel like I can be read as easily as book - and not one that is particularly well written.

"Is mystery a staple in your life?" I asked, not knowing any other way to keep things going without completely changing the subject (I hadn't prepared any topics of conversation to bring up, although the creation of which should have somehow factored into my weekend but didn't). I personally felt she'd be more suited to film noir at this point in our conversation, the way she spoke of mystery, and hoped that she didn't ask me to find some lover who had run out on her. I was more suited to play a detective's accountant rather than a Private Eye (even though I have always loved the play on words between PI, Private Eye and Private Investigator).

"The easy answer to that question is that mystery is a staple in everyone's lives, I guess," Gabriella said, pulling her lunch from her bag. "The long form answer is a little too complex for first thing on a Monday. I've only had one coffee and all of that caffeinated energy has been expended on work tasks already."

"Especially after a weekend wedding out of town for a friend of a friend," I offered. I was curious how her weekend went, but didn't want to pry. Wait, who am I kidding? I really wanted to know. I wanted her to share as much as possible so I could find some way in which we related to each other's personalities.

"Very true!" she sighed, extracting an overstuffed sandwich from her glass food transportation container. I took a second to consider if it was a better method than my plastic baggies. "It was a well planned ceremony and all of that, but I always feel strangely about being at such an intimate life event when I barely know the people involved."

"I've always been confused by the people who feel a need to invite people they technically know but never see and aren't close to," I answered, changing my posture to mock a fictional groom. *"Yes, but we simply must invite my third cousin, even though I have never met her due to her living on the other side of the country, otherwise there will be an uproar in the family."* The voice came out more snooty than I had anticipated, but I ran with it. Rich and snotty people would invite relatives they've never met, right?

"Exactly!" she giggled again. I could get very used to hearing that delightful sound, especially when I played some relevant part in its creation. "It was nice that they let Anna bring me, since she gets really self-conscious at these types of things - not to mention a wedding is an awkward high-stress date, and she isn't seeing anyone romantically at the moment." She paused to sample her sandwich. "I guess lots of people try to plan a small party and there are inevitable tag-ons."

"It's nice that you were able to help your friend, though." I don't know if I would feel too keen about attending a wedding for people I didn't know, but then again I don't think Figaro has any engaged friends right now, so I am in the clear.

"She's wonderful, so I don't mind giving up a weekend for her once in a while."

The inevitable conversation lull rushed in, choking my brain of anything interesting to add. The more I tried to think of something to say, the further away my imaginary box of conversation topics floated. I could vividly picture this blue velvet box with its own set of white feathered wings as it was becoming a speck on the horizon when Gabriella saved the conversation and brought me back to the current moment in reality.

"How was your weekend?" Gabriella offered, finishing the first half of her sandwich. I made note of this, as though it were a time cue akin to turning over an hour glass filled with sand. When the sand ran out, so would my time with Gabriella. In this instance, though, I could always stop her from eating the sandwich if only I could distract her with intelligent or fascinating conversation - if only I could form either of those concepts into a coherent sentence.

"My weekend was pretty usual, although not as productive as I'd like." I was able to breath again; words came out of my mouth once more. They weren't terribly inspired, but being able to speak words that formed a full sentence felt good after watching all of my thoughts get dragged away in a winged blue velvet box by the vortex of silence.

"Writers' block?" Her sandwich was disappearing at an alarming rate, which made me feel as though our time together after a weekend of waiting was coming to a very quick and unsatisfying close.

"Yeah, I wasn't able to get any more of the story out." I suddenly realized I hadn't touched my food, and my tea had grown cold in my hands. The weight of the mug was still doing the job of keeping my hands from shaking; however, I didn't care to test if they would be noticeably jittery should I take them from the calming talisman.

"Just keep working at it. If it doesn't come easy, it is probably worth continuing." I caught her eyes, and surprised myself by not immediately breaking the gaze. "What would motivate you to keep at it?" she inquired.

I swallowed a large portion of the leftovers I'd brought for lunch, taking care to really chew the mouthful. Maybe the fact that my lunch was still on the table would help keep her in the conversation longer. "I'm pretty indecisive when it comes to what my characters should do," I replied.

"Do you work better with deadlines?" she asked, starting to tuck her lunch items back her in bag. My brilliant plan of using leftovers as a distraction was failing miserably.

"I guess it helps a little to know that I am expected to have something done sooner rather than later." I really wanted her to leave later rather than sooner, though.

"Then let me offer you some help." She unfolded her long legs and stood, pulling a card from the back pocket of her perfectly tailored trousers and quickly printed something on the back. "You can call me to arrange a dinner date once you've written another chapter. My cell number is on the back." The card made its way into my hand, but I don't remember raising my fingers to meet hers. I unconsciously checked my extended limb for tremors before scanning the information on her card. I don't think the shake was noticeable, but I kept my hand moving so the stationary position wouldn't give my terror tremor away.

"What if my writers' block doesn't go away for a while?" I asked as she turned back toward her secret door. I just wanted to salvage any remaining time I could squeeze out of this meeting.

"Then I guess I don't make a very good muse," she replied over her shoulder, and disappeared.

I need to start writing about Randell and Cynthia again. I keep checking to make sure her card is still in my pocket, and have already emailed myself with all of the information on her card, just in case the card somehow jumps ship or gets left in my pants on laundry day. I don't think that recording our lunch together counts as a chapter, so I cannot call her until my characters do something of note. As per usual, Figaro is just looking at me with that adorably dumb grin that is of absolutely no help.

"I don't make it a habit to stay in one town too long if there isn't anything keeping me there," Cynthia started. "So I guess we better talk about what we are doing."

"I thought that was kind of obvious," Randell joked, sliding his hand over her bare skin.

"You know what I mean," she replied, playfully swatting his fingers, but not wanting them to leave the warm flesh of her back. His fingers tensed, massaging the tired muscles in her shoulders.

"I don't know what to say," Randell admitted. He didn't want to ask her to stay if she wanted to leave, but he didn't want her to go thinking he didn't like having her around. He hadn't been in a relationship situation since his parents died, and that was just the adolescent version of love. He'd broken up with that girl because she was too smothering, as though he couldn't get over his parent's death and needed help in every aspect of his life. He didn't know how these things were supposed to go. He didn't even know if he loved Cynthia, although the fact that he felt drawn back to town each week to see her had to count for something. He couldn't ask her to stay, in case he was only experiencing lust. He just knew that he was enjoying what they had.

"I'm not asking for much," she continued. "I just don't like overstaying my welcome. If you think you'll get tired of me, I'd rather leave before that happens."

"Is that what happened in the last town?"

"The last town was not my usual story," she curled onto her side to look at him. His gaze stayed on the ceiling. "He didn't treat me well, and I took my opportunity to leave. It was that simple."

"Why do I get the feeling that everything is more complicated than you let on?" he joked. He didn't have a lot of experience, but was led to believe that few things were simple when more than one person was involved.

"It was simple on my end. I don't know how he felt about it, because I didn't stick around to ask. But he had at least one other girl he was seeing," she said. "He thought I didn't know, but he never gave me enough credit."

"If I felt it would help, I'd say that I'm not seeing anyone else, but I guess you already figured that out," Randell joked, taking in the silence of his cabin, and the small sounds from the woods outside.

***

My fingers felt an interesting paradox of rough but slippery as I checked the number over and over before I dialled the digits. There hadn't been any rules made as to how long the chapter had to be before I was allowed to call Gabriella. I took full advantage of that logic.

"Hello?" She answered on the second ring, her voice light, as though it was far away. I guess it actually was, and was momentarily distracted by marvelling at technology. The line was silent for slightly too long, and she repeated her salutation slightly louder, likely thinking the phone signal had failed.

"Oh, hi, Gabriella," I stammered. "It's Andy."

"Does this mean you wrote another chapter?" she cooed. I could feel her attention focus directly on me, even though the phone. Usually something like that would make me feel nervous. Right now, it made me feel intensely nervous. I tilted the mouthpiece of the phone away from my face so I could take deep breaths without sounding like a psycho killer from her end of the conversation.

"I was able to get the cursor moving on my computer, yes." She didn't say I had to write a brilliant chapter before calling her, but I felt like the quality of my creation might come under inspection.

"You don't sound satisfied," she observed. I pictured her lounging on an elegant, comfortable couch with a fluffy blanket and a glass of wine. I don't even know if she likes red wine, but that is what she was drinking in my mind. It matched her distracting lips.

"That's the thing about writing - it is hard to know if what you are putting down is any good," I replied, closing my eyes to more vividly picture her home scene. Somehow the visual distraction was making it easier to concentrate on the words in the conversation.

"Maybe you'll let me read it sometime?" she asked. I pictured her shoes kicked off next to the couch, and dinner in the oven. My fantasy of her included excellent culinary skills. My stomach rumbled to remind me that I hadn't eaten yet, although Figaro's unimpressed look from the coffee table was enough to remind me that neither of us had had dinner.

"When it is finished, maybe you can read it, if you want," I started. "Assuming I don't chicken out. And assuming it is ever finished."

"Am I that scary?" she chuckled. I delighted in the sound and pictured the notes as flowing wisps of smoke that travelled through her phone and into my mind.

"No, it isn't you I am scared of," I replied, although that wasn't altogether correct. There was no rule that I had to tell the whole truth (when the part of the truth that I am withholding would only serve as embarrassment instead of helpful fact). "It has more to do with whatever I am writing not being good enough for people to spend their time reading it. I wouldn't want to get your hopes up, just to have you realize you'd wasted all that time and energy on being excited and then reading something that stinks."

"I can understand that," she replied. "I used to get really nervous about my design choices at the beginning of my career, and was constantly second-guessing myself." There was a muffled sound of movement on the other end of the phone. I pictured her sitting up so she could reach and drink from her wine glass more comfortably than in her semi-recumbent posture. "I'd love to read it when you are ready for me to do so, how's that?"

"I can definitely live with that." Figaro started to head butt me, and I suddenly realized that I was meant to be asking her to dinner. Figaro didn't have to be asked to dinner, but definitely wanted it, pronto. I hadn't even rehearsed what to say or how to say it, and suddenly my thoughts began to whirl away, not pausing to let me in on the secret of what to do next.

"I feel like I sort of put you on the spot with mentioning a dinner date," her words seemed farther away than before. I started to worry that I might be blacking out at the prospect of her taking back her offer of going on a date with me. "We could skip the whole conversation of where to go if you want." I definitely started to have blurred vision while the rest of her sentence resonated in my head. "If you would prefer to come over to my apartment on Friday night for dinner instead, that would work, as I love entertaining guests." My mind teetered on the edge of disappointment before falling back into reality.

"That sounds like a very good plan," I breathed a sigh of relief, and hoped it was much less audible on her end of the line. "Can I bring anything?" My mind was doing flips of joy for somehow dodging the responsibility of picking "the perfect first date restaurant".

"A bottle of red wine would be an excellent addition to the meal I'm planning - you aren't allergic to anything, are you?" Her voice was closer again, as though she'd just finished her sip of wine, replaced her long stemmed glass on the table and settled back into her couch.

"No dietary restrictions," I replied. I was suddenly struck with amazement at guessing subtle details of her life, as I'd pictured her as inclined to great culinary skills with a taste for red wine. Could some of my fantasy actually be reality when it comes to her? Or was I simply deciding the meaning behind some of her verbal patterns based on the way she was situated in my mind? I tossed the image aside for a moment to grasp at another question as a means of keeping her on the line a little while longer. "Do you have a favourite varietal?"

"Oh, look at you," she giggled. "Not many people would think to ask which red wine grapes someone prefers."

"I would prefer to do this as well as possible," I admitted, and immediately thought I might have been too bold. I felt as stupid as a fish trying to climb a tree. I became all too grateful that we were discussing this over the phone, where she couldn't see me blush and start to sweat. I now had only a few days to get that under control before arriving at her apartment and trying desperately to not screw things up.

"Just breath, Andy," she offered. "I'll likely see you in the lobby around lunch time for the next few days, but if not, see you on Friday. I'll make sure you have my address."

I think we said goodbye, but I honestly don't recall. Perhaps I have a mental block about stopping conversations with her. Maybe we don't actually say goodbye and I just assume we do because that is the societal norm. Either way, I don't really mind - I have somehow lucked into a date with a beautiful, elegant woman. It is time to research techniques to get rid of nervousness. It is also time for me to feed my damn cat, before he attacks me just so he has something on which to feast.

*** *** ***

I arrived at my desk this morning and found a handwritten card:

Andy,

I found out early this morning that I'll be out of the office on business for a few days, but didn't want you to think that I was avoiding our little lunch meetings. I'll be back sometime on Friday, but figured I might not cross paths with you, and definitely still want your company on Friday night. Don't forget to bring your favourite varietal of red wine, as I like them all. See you around 7pm.

- Gabriella

Her address was below. I looked it up online and it turns out that it is actually rather close to my own apartment, but it is just situated on a side street onto which I have never ventured. I don't think I've ever received a card to remind me about a date before. I think it is classy, with a little quirk, which sums up how I see Gabriella in general. I don't know if not seeing her before the date will make me more or less nervous - all I know for certain is that I will be nervous, and I will bring a bottle of wine, and I will hope for the best. If I want to make it through this, I cannot dwell on what could go wrong, but I also have a problem wishing too hard for things to go right. I don't even actually know if she finds me attractive - she could have just been helping cultivate my creativity, because she enjoys her creative life style so much. I guess I'll have to spell it out and tell her that I think she's beautiful, and see how it goes from there. Will words come when the time does? I guess it will be a mystery.

***

There is nothing quite like the morning after sharing a couple of bottles of wine with a beautiful woman; and sometimes it is difficult to put those events into coherent sentences that really capture the evening after the experience has concluded. I'll get to writing about my evening with Gabriella, and what happened, in a moment, but I need to talk about the reason why it feels like there is sludge attempting to pump its way through my veins. I've avoided this problem for years, but it caught up to me. Even Figaro has looked at me with disgust already today, although most of his looks centre around being some form of superior being that I must wait on like a slave.

I am very hungover. I fear that I cannot express my displeasure at this feeling as clearly as I would like, as the wine is still floating my brain back and forth in my skull, but I will try, if only for my own amusement. Most things I do are only for my own amusement, so this experience shouldn't be any different.

When I first woke up, opening my eyes seemed like an impossible task. I stayed in darkness, almost comforted by it, and knowing there was nothing but bright, blinding light outside my eye lids. Previous Me was an absolute genius and didn't turn off the lights before passing out. Opening my eyes did not seem to be in any way necessary to my immediate survival, so I put it off as long as my bladder would allow. Figaro sped this process along by jumping on my stomach. I decided he knew that I was in pain and was getting back at me for some perceived slight. My cat appears to be a vengeful cat. I gingerly opened one eye, and then the other, which resulted in immediate defeat. I gave up, and I think I might have fallen back to sleep for a brief interlude from the pounding in my veins. The vacation was swift and I look back to it fondly. Figaro camped out on my abdomen, as though he had finally decided that he enjoyed cuddling with me like I had been trying to convince him for years. My fingers are full of jitters even as I type this, which is infuriating, as I keep having to go back and retype due to errors. I want this account to be precise, so I never, ever make this stupid mistake ever again in my entire life.

I was forced to open both eyes again, at least one at a time, so I could navigate my way to a standing position and ricochet my way down the hall and into the bathroom. I cannot recall another time in my life where relieving myself seemed like such an utter chore. If it wasn't an activity that pretty much needed to continue to completion once started, I might have considered a nap mid way through the process. Had I previously invented a way to nap while standing up, this definitely would have occurred en route to the bathroom.

Once I finished, the act of crawling all the way back down the long hallway to my bed seemed much more effort than trying to kill the pain with a long, hot shower, so I started the water and wriggled out of last night's clothing. If I had bothered to close the door, the bathroom would have been filled with steam by the time I figured out how to detach my socks from my feet. I didn't invent the perks of the bachelor lifestyle, but I do occasionally cash in on them. I give absolutely no care to if Figaro sees me naked. He can stare all he wants, as long as he keeps his distance.

I leaned my poor, mistreated body against the wall of the shower stall and let the water cascade over my skin until it started to run cold. I made a cape out of one towel, and wrapped the other around my waist for the long trek back to the warmth of my calling bed.

And it was only then that I realized the sun wasn't even up yet, a subject that was masked by the fact that Previous Me had left the bedroom light on, and potential sources of bright light are intermixed when your brain is trying to explode. It was only 6:45am. Why did my body decide I needed to be up so early on a Saturday morning?! Clearly, I need sleep, so why didn't I just sleep through this utter hell?

My body is a prankster, and one hell of a jerk sometimes. Maybe it is taking lessons from my evil cat.

I guess it is my own fault; I should have realized that I haven't actually had much alcohol to drink in a really long time, and that my body would not be the most appreciative due to a low tolerance for alcohol. Especially since we started the bottle before dinner was ready. And especially since I brought two bottles of wine, just in case I made the wrong selection at the liquor store. It also probably didn't help that I had neglected eating all day because I was busy with work and trying to not overthink what might unfold during the evening.

Last night, after ensuring that Figaro had a feast of his own for whenever he decided to awake from his very important nap, I walked to Gabriella's from my apartment. I was very careful to make sure I was neither late nor horrendously early. I had to pause a couple of times along the way, because my legs kept speeding up with excitement. I felt like I was sweating, but kept checking and not noticing anything too severe. I made sure to wipe my face and hands while I took the elevator up to her floor.

She opened the door wearing a smile and a gorgeous, deep purple dress. My hands were full (a bottle in each hand) and I didn't know really what to do besides say hello from her threshold and wait for her to invite me in. I put the bottles out in front of me as a peace offering.

"I couldn't decide, and didn't know which one you would prefer," I tried to explain as she gracefully took the wine bottles from my slippery fingers and left me to close the door I had just come through.

"Both are nice, Andy," she replied, motioning me toward the coat rack with her elbow as I danced around her entry way, not knowing where to go. "Thank you."

"It's my pleasure," I said, depositing my coat, peeling off each shoe with the opposing foot, and following the sound of her voice around the corner. Her apartment had an amazing living room and kitchen space, with a gorgeous view of the city below. I was also delighted to notice a rather luxurious looking couch with a cosy blanket tucked away on one side. I remembered back to our phone conversation and decided that the girl inside my head might be more like the girl ahead of me than I assumed. I reminded myself to try to not get ahead of where the evening was, and just enjoy the woman who was here physically, not the one who was in my head. "You have a beautiful home."

"Thank you," I heard from over my shoulder. She had already gone back to whatever she was making, which smelled amazing. "Sorry if I seem distracted, I just wanted to make sure this sauce doesn't burn."

"Can I help with anything?" I asked, secretly hoping that whatever task she doled out to me wasn't too complicated. It would calm my nerves if I had a task in which to busy myself.

"You can open the first bottle of wine - and honestly, you choose. There is no wrong answer when it comes to red wine." A cork screw appeared on the counter just before she spun around to attend to something else on the other side of the kitchen. I made a small show for my own amusement of playing "eeny, meany, miney mo," before selecting the bottle closest to me. By the time I removed the cork, two glasses appeared on the counter in front of me.

"To what shall we toast?" I asked, coming around the island that separated us and handing her a full glass of wine. The light shone through both glasses and created two dancing red orbs on the countertop.

"How about muses, creativity and fine food?" She offered, quickly wiping her slender fingers on a dish towel before accepting the glass. The red light orbs bounced around the countertops, cabinets and floor depending on where we held the glasses. I found this distraction oddly soothing, as the orbs seemed to float and flow around the kitchen.

"To muses, creativity and fine food," I accepted. We looked each other in the eye as we clinked glasses, and each took a sip. An unfamiliar texture danced around my tongue, as though I was trying to remember a name that lived at the tip of my tongue but was too shy to be spoken. Did I mention it had been a while since I last drunk alcohol?

"That's perfect, Andy," she said, setting her glass down in order to have both hands free to put a dish in the oven. "It will go great with this lasagna - old family recipe, so I hope you like it, and no, I cannot share the secret to the sauce." She sent a teasing smile my way as she finished wiping down the counter and grabbed her glass of wine. "It will take a little while to bake, but we can adjourn to the living room instead of standing around my kitchen."

"Lead the way," I said, ensuring a firm grip on the neck of the open wine bottle. She trod lightly around the island and settled into one end of the couch, and I fiddled with putting the wine bottle on the coffee table while I tried to figure out how close I should sit. She distracted me with a question, and I eventually sunk into the middle of the couch - not too close, but close enough to really look at her.

"What is your book about?" She asked, facing me directly and leaning her back into the arm of the couch. I took a sip from my wine glass and held it close, scared of dropping it or spilling it if I got too animated.

"It is really hard to say, at this point," I admitted. I tried to create a synopsis in my head that would be interesting, but kept thinking that "a social recluse meets a pretty woman" sounded too much like a cop out. To be honest, it might be, but I didn't start writing about Randell and Cynthia so I could bring them up in conversation. It also sounded alarmingly like my current situation, although I'm not half as fit as Randell, and Gabriella is far darker in hair and eye colour than Cynthia, not to mention they have vastly different personalities.

"Is it full of mystery?" she giggled, curling her legs under her body and emphasising the last word in her question in a joking tone. I knew her question was a throwback to our previous conversation on the subject, and felt a smile spread across my own face.

"There is some intrigue, so far," I admitted, "but I don't really know how to take it to the next step."

"One foot in front of the other," she said, supplying the easiest answer to a difficult problem. I took a moment to enjoy that she looked well dressed up in her purple dress, but simultaneously casual due to her bare feet. I restrained myself from peeking next to the couch for discarded shoes, like the ones I had pictured during our phone conversation. Finding exactly what I pictured would likely be more eerie than exciting.

"I'm not very good with quick decisions," I replied, diverting my eyes to the wine I was swirling around in my glass. "I take my time, which doesn't make for quick progress."

"What was that quote: something to do with if it is written well, it is not written fast and if it is written fast it is not written well?" She sipped from her glass and a flash of my fantasy of her over the phone popped into my head again. "Just don't think it over any more than it actually needs, or you'll never finish, and it isn't about being perfect, but being complete in that moment."

"Do you teach classes in inspiration on the side?" I joked, fully meaning it as a compliment, but worried I would come off sounding sappy or as though my aim was to put her down. She laughed. I took it as a good sign that I wasn't offending her. I felt like I had dodged another awkward situation bullet.

"No, not as of yet, although I'll spout my opinions on creativity to anyone who will hear them." Finishing the last sip in her glass, she rose to check on dinner.

"Should I top up your glass?" I asked, not wanting to assume anything, although my glass was now dry as well. I took her smile and nod as a hearty yes and drained the bottle into our glasses. My glass was a little too full so I tried to slurp a bit out while her back was turned so I wouldn't look indecorous. I should have known that covering my ass by drinking more was a bad move, but by this point the alcohol was already in my system, impairing my judgement.

"I hope you aren't starving; this recipe takes a little while, but it is well worth the wait," she called as she wandered back from the kitchen. The truth was that even though I had been too nervous to eat much all day, but didn't really feel hungry. I was starting to feel warm, though, which I now assume was caused by the wine. I would have checked to see if I was sweating, but she was looking at me again, so I just allowed myself to get lost in returning her smile.

"I'm a patient guy," I replied, realizing I was silent a little too long. That's what happens when you get stuck in your own head. Even though I get stuck there often, it seems like the exit is a moving target. I get stuck, I panic, I flail to get out once I realize I am stuck and it always feels like it takes an eternity for me to get free and move away from that specific pit. Sometimes I stop and take notes about it, and wonder why it is there, and it sucks me back in again and I cannot seem to function in a normal social setting without feeling as though people around me must think I am letting my mind wander because they are boring. How I would love to explain that I am actually a prisoner in my own head, and not at all being rude, but rather that I am kept captive - but that would result in people thinking I was crazy, and I picture them backing away slowly rather than helping me out of my mind traps.

"So, besides fabric acquisition and your part time gig of being a muse, what do you do for fun?" I asked as Gabriella folded herself back into her corner of the couch. I attribute the playfulness of the second half of that list of her career paths to my rising level of wine consumption, but I felt pretty proud that I let down my guard and flirted a little. At least, I think it was flirting. That was my intention, but I have many steps to go before I can declare myself a master of that art. It could be a lifelong goal that I might never achieve.

"I spend a fair amount of time doing things I find relaxing - reading, watching procedural television shows: basically anything I can do from the comfort of my couch with a glass of wine and a warm blanket." She took another sip and let the glass hover near her lips, as though she was considering either another sip or another item to add to her list.

"I have a small love/hate relationship with crime shows," I confessed. I had to pry my eyes from her lips, as they now seemed to be demanding my full attention.

"Let me guess," she jumped in, thankfully oblivious to my short lived staring contest with her lips. "You love watching them, but once you realize you spent the whole day caught in their hypnotic trap, you feel guilty?"

"Did I miss the portion of your biography that included the fact that you are a mind reader?" If I didn't like her company so much, I might have considered being bewildered or taken aback by her accuracy. If she was able to guess this about me and still wanted me in her house, I felt like odds were in my favour.

"Oh, now, I am just speaking from personal experience," she giggled. I momentarily reflected that her being a mind reader wouldn't work to my advantage anyway, unless she found anxiety endearing. "I used to feel so guilty after bingeing on TV, but I finally realized that it was time well spent because I enjoy doing it, and my enjoyment is important."

"That's the way I am trying to look at it, too," I replied. Her gaze conveyed that she didn't really believe me. "Macaw - erm, uh," I suddenly realized that I had come dangerously close to telling this woman that I have a therapist, which isn't great first date material, in my humble opinion. I cleared my throat. "My, uh, cousin pointed out the whole theory of 'you're no good to anybody else if you aren't good to yourself'. I'm not there yet, but I am working on getting rid of that guilt that comes with being, quote unquote selfish." Dear creator, help me, but I actually used two-handed air quotes around the word selfish. I immediately blamed the wine, even though the glass had tried to restrict my fingers on my right hand so I couldn't make such an embarrassing gesture.

"One of the best things you can do is spend time doing whatever you like," Gabriella quipped, quaffing another sip of wine. If she was just politely ignoring my bumbling idiot shtick, she was very good at doing so. "I sound like a self help book, but I meant that sincerely."

"I'm sure you did," I replied, following her lead and taking another sip to fill the dead air. Underneath the terror I was feeling, I was enjoying being with her. Another wave of fear lived below that - one of wondering if she was enjoying herself. It felt like one of those "if you have to ask, then the answer probably isn't in your favour" moments.

"Are you sure there isn't anything I can do to help with dinner?" I asked, defaulting to politeness in place of knowing where else to take the conversation. If you can't say anything nice, you probably aren't supposed to be in that situation, I thought to myself.

"Oh, I should check on that - it should be done soon." She leapt from her place with endearing grace, narrowly missing her coffee table and keeping her wine glass upright and unspilled in the process. I clenched my glass in reflex, but made sure to release my finger vice before it cracked her glassware.

Dinner really was worth the wait. Perhaps I have been eating lazy bachelor food for way too long, considering a little effort could result in this delicious feast. I actually did want to ask her about the sauce, but refrained from doing so due to her previous comment. I did, however tell her that it was amazing.

There was too much delicious lasagna to focus on in-depth conversation, but I asked her about her work meetings and was satisfied that they went well, even if they did keep her out of the office, and thus out of conversational range of my lunchtime people watching sessions. I helped her clean up the kitchen until she kicked me out, adamant that she could load the dishwasher herself, and that letting guests do chores was not the mark of a good hostess. She said it in a joking voice, similar to my snotty groom routine. I didn't mind being kicked out the kitchen when it was done so playfully.

I noticed a chess set in the corner of her living room, set up and ready for a game, and wandered over to inspect it, since I was of no use in her kitchen. I had never really played a lot of chess, considering it was a two person game that I cannot seem to get Figaro to master, but I knew the rules.

"Do you play?" she asked, coming up behind me and handing me my abandoned glass of wine. I briefly wondered how long I had been contemplating the chess board. I was vaguely aware that the second bottle was now emptied into our glasses, but focused more on the fact that she was asking me a question. My brain swayed slightly before recalling the appropriate information to form a response.

"No, not much," I replied, worried I would be challenged to a game that I would lose miserably. Then again, I wouldn't hate the experience, as I was very much enjoying spending time with her.

"Are you being truthful or are you some sort of chess shark, just waiting to take me in for the kill?" She giggled again, the wine glass making an appearance on her lips once more.

"I'd be classified closer to a chess jellyfish," I replied. "I just kind of move around, not really knowing where I am going." I did what would have been an embarrassing imitation of a jellyfish if it hadn't amused her as much as it did. I gained another giggle. I wanted to keep winning them, like small, verbal trophies.

"I could teach you sometime, if you like," she said, catching her breath from her outbreak of adorable giggles and fiddling with one of the pawns before returning it to its starting place on the board.

"Let me guess - after I write another chapter?" I asked, unable to keep the smile from my face. I was about 90 percent sure that I was flirting successfully, which gave me a momentary boost of confidence that felt foreign, yet comfortable, like a new couch.

"Only if that would be helpful, Andy." She moved slightly closer to me as she shifted her weight from one foot to the other, and our faces were inches apart. I breathed as deeply as my lungs would allow, but seemed unable to take in any air. I met her gaze. She didn't look away.

"To muses," I finally said, raising my glass. We drank deep, and I couldn't help but drain my glass. She did the same with hers. I delicately relieved her of her glass, feeling the sway of the wine within my chest. I placed both of our glasses on the ledge next to us that served as a bookshelf over the chess table. This action broke our gaze for only a moment. When my eyes flicked back to hers, she hadn't seemed to have diverted her gaze. Slowly, almost too afraid to try, I lifted my hand to her chin and tilted her face up, slightly, and brought my lips to hers.

Kissing is something difficult to describe with total accuracy. The actual physical sensation, completely detached from the emotional activity, can be described with words indicating pressure levels, moisture, texture or heat. Her lips were soft on mine, and didn't flinch away as I moved mine to explore hers. I lost all sense of time. The room began to lilt back and forth, but we remained still, inches from each other and only connected by my lips on hers and my fingers on her jaw line. I felt her hand cup my side, and I pulled her closer - calmly, slowly, focusing more on the kiss than the touch of fingers on fine fabric.

We slowly broke apart, so gradually that I wasn't able to pinpoint the moment between when the kiss stopped and when we became just two people standing very closely.

"I hope that was alright," I stammered quietly, wanting to continue holding her, and wanting to kiss her again if she would permit it.

"I would say," she began, catching my eyes with hers. "That was quite enjoyable."

I could have died happy just then. I'm not sure if it was fortunate or unfortunate that the universe had a different plan for me. It definitely feels extremely one-sided since my brain already has the memory of what came next.

Her body weight shifted and moved away from mine, returning her giraffe legs to a curled position under her body on the couch. I stood by the chess table, unmoved from the spot where we kissed, and watched her through the low light. Was she retreating? Did she want me to follow? Despite years of observing people, I have rarely been one to understand slight social or physical cues. I felt pulled to follow her motion, and placed myself on the couch, closer to her than before, but not quite touching.

"Did I do something wrong?" I asked, at a loss for where to go from our current moment. I felt a need for validation that our evening was going as well as it seemed to be going in my wine-soaked brain.

"No, not at all," she assured, keeping her eyes averted. "I haven't been completely forthcoming with you."

My heart nearly stopped in my chest. This is where everything that feels like it is going right is taken away from me. I always told myself that it was a coincidence, but it has happened so many times that I don't know if I can ignore that it is a pattern. I had no other course of action besides awaiting my fate.

I don't really care to write about this any more. I'm going to try to nap. It seems backwards, considering the sun is finally starting to rise, but I have put down as much as I can stomach right now. Needless to say, I stopped for more alcohol on my way home, which was not the most intelligent move, but it seemed to make sense at the time. It always seems easier to drink when you've already been drinking.

***

I would call that one of the least successful naps I have ever attempted. I believe that I had moments of sleep, but I feel like I spent more time waking up than I did actually sleeping. At least Figaro calmed down a little bit instead of constantly trampling all over my slightly animated corpse.

I should have known that she has a boyfriend. Why did I go in for that kiss? For that matter, why did she let me? I cannot recall an experience outside of grade school where I have been anywhere near this embarrassed, which is applicable considering I was a kid who was pantsed more than once.

"I'm sort of in a relationship," she spat out, curling up into a tighter ball on her end of the couch. I leaned away, unaware of how to extract myself from her personal space without the step of actually lifting myself up and moving farther along the couch. I guess she didn't really invite me over because she liked me. She really was just being kind. I should have listened to my instinct that no one thinks of me in a romantic way, but my desperate hope ran away with the notion that I might be wrong.

"I should leave," I stated formally, trying to arranged my limbs so that I could stand, as that was the first step to finding my coat, getting out the door and finding my way to any other space so my stink of embarrassment could dissipate.

"I didn't mean to upset you," I distantly heard her say. A hand with slender fingers landed on my forearm and gripped firmly. "I just really like you and wanted to get to know you."

"I don't know what to say." I felt physically trapped. The wine pressed down on my body, and I didn't know how to get out from under the light touch that was starting to feel heavier and heavier on my arm. "For the record, I had no idea you have a boyfriend, or I wouldn't have made an ass of myself. At least not as much of an ass of myself."

"I should have said something earlier," she admitted. "But it is complicated." It took everything I had not to spit an angry retort at her. I channeled that energy into finding my way onto my feet, tearing loose of her grip. I still couldn't look at her. I don't know if I will be able to look at her again, even in passing at our work building. I might have to avoid the lobby of the building during usual commute times and start eating my lunch at my desk, because any activity of people watching that includes seeing her is no longer something I can take pleasure in.

It isn't as though I assumed we were contracted to be together or anything. I just feel mislead, and since I acted on feelings that could have been stopped if she had bothered to give me the relevant information, I feel stupid. It would have been the easiest thing in the world to drop something about her boyfriend into any of the handful of conversations we've had, especially when she invited me to not only call her for a dinner date, but suggest it take place at her home. I think the card led me to believe that she was more interested in me than she actually is.

Next time I'll ask. Next time I will trust my instincts that say things are too good to be true. Next time I will try to not care too hard, because everything tends to be all in my head, and it isn't fair to expect my life to work out like my fantasies. I got an alarming amount of things right about her, and even more alarming things wrong.

I need a break to stretch my back and make sure the cat isn't plotting something heinous in the other room...

■ ■

My phone, which I somehow managed to leave in my kitchen sink last night, has a couple of missed class from her number. I'm too exhausted and upset to even think about calling her without causing myself further embarrassment. Like Randell, I don't need her pity. Like Randell, I just want to be left alone. I don't think I'll be able to work on his story, because my heart just isn't into creative energy. I'm mostly just writing this down as a reminder to myself that sometimes things go very wrong, and I need to keep my armour shiny so I don't get hurt in the future.

I just reread that, and I sound horribly melodramatic, which makes me just want to give up and spend the rest of the weekend in bed. I told myself I'm not allowed to erase anything I write in here, but I really don't want to sound so pathetic. Not to mention, I am no knight in shining armour.

I enjoyed it for the brief amount of time it lasted, so at least I have that to hold onto. She said she liked the kiss as well, but my inner pessimist suspects that she was just being polite. The point is moot, considering it will never happen again.

***

The first day back at the office after my humiliation was an absolute nightmare. I felt like I had to sneak around a building that I used to have free reign in - and not in the fun way I created to keep myself amused and moving around the office. I sped through the lobby both times I had to cross it - once going in and once leaving - and ate lunch at my desk. I didn't pack a lunch, so my feast was food from the vending machine at the end of the cubical row that I am sure hasn't been restocked in quite some time. It also felt like everyone was looking at me, like my humiliation was a stink that just wouldn't fade, and they somehow all knew that my weekend didn't go very well. Does shame have a scent, like a disgusting aftershave? If not, can I market that some how?

I kept telling myself that it was all in my head. More often than not, that is the situation. I kept telling myself that if I ignored it all, it would go away. I was telling myself that when a hand tapped me on the shoulder while I was within the sanctity of my desk space, something that did not occur often nor was it generally invited. I briefly wondered how she knew how to find me, but remembered her hand written invitation to the night from which I still haven't recovered.

"Hi Andy," she started. I could feel people looking my way, even through the cubicle walls. I didn't want to cause a scene, and people were probably already curious as to why a beautiful woman was talking to me. New occurrences are always something intriguing to talk about in this social hell hole, and the boring finance guy talking to a beautiful and mysterious woman was not an event they had seen before. I didn't need a public rejection or demonstration of pity to act as a follow up to the private one that encouraged the most draining weekend in recent memory, and I wasn't about to let that happen.

I made sure my voice was low, so she would have to stoop to hear me, and other people wouldn't have a chance of prying into our conversation. "What are you doing here?"

"I was hoping to see you in the lobby at lunch, so I could explain-"

I cut her off. "You already explained. You are with someone else, and I was just a complete asshat to think that you were interested in me."

"That's not it at all!" Her voice rose too loud for my taste, and I heard the normal sounds of my office dull. People were taking notice. I had to get her out of there.

"Can we talk in the stairwell?" I asked, although I was not giving her any time to accept or decline the offer. I was already leading her there and out of the sight of the hawk eyes that followed our every move. I found the door, tucked away in a corner, and rushed inside the cold, cement stairway. There was a slight echo, but the door closed and vast silence softened the reverberation.

"I left a couple of messages," she started. I no longer felt the need to jump immediately to cover the ends of her sentences, and let this one hang longer than absolutely necessary.

"I know. I didn't listen to them," I admitted, proud that I hadn't given into the little blinking envelope on my phone. I had thought of deleting them, but the only way to do that was to start playing each message, and I had not wanted to hear her voice again over the weekend. I wasn't that thrilled about hearing it now. She was forcing it upon me at that moment, so I briefly reflected that I would probably have the courage to delete the jailed voice mail messages after our meeting was over. It would give me some busy work to do while warding off the rubberneckers in my office. If I did things that were uninteresting for long enough, they would eventually lose interest and move on with their work.

"I wish you had. I'm so sorry, Andy, I didn't mean to hurt you like that, or at all." She was finding it hard to make eye contact, at least in the few seconds that I let myself look her way.

"You could have told me sooner," I blurted. "It would have been nice to know that you have a boyfriend instead of making an ass of myself."

"The situation is a little more complicated than that," she began again. I didn't want to hear how she justified cheating on him. I'd been cheated on by an alarmingly high percentage of my girlfriends, and no one deserves that. Why is honesty so hard to come by?

"What makes this case so different from any other time a woman invites a man over, cooks him a meal, asks him to bring wine, kisses him and then tells him that she is unavailable?" At this point, I couldn't contain my hurt feelings anymore. I really wanted to know why she thought she was so special.

"I know I didn't go about this the right way, and I don't want to make any excuses, but I assure you that this is a case that has no pre-plotted basis and no manual on how I am supposed to feel." I chanced another glance in her direction. She had tears in her eyes, and I'm no expert, but they seemed genuine. She lifted her head to look back at me, and didn't bother to wipe her eyes. "He's been in a coma for 14 months now, and I don't know if he is ever going to wake up."

I didn't have time to form a coherent thought before Marty, one of the party guys from my office, burst into the stairwell. "We have that meeting in five minutes, Andy," he said, eyeing Gabriella up and down in a way that was far from subtle.

"Thanks, Marty," I replied as an automatic response. He didn't leave, and was fortunately oblivious to the fact that Gabriella had been in tears when he interrupted. She had turned her back to him, but he still seemed to be enjoying the view. "I'll be there in a moment." Marty slowly slunk back through the door, making what I could only assume were rude gestures. The office noises faded as the door slammed shut.

"Sorry about him," I apologized, taking a step toward Gabriella. Her eyes were rimmed with red, but her face was dry. She attempted a smile, I assumed out of reflexive courtesy. We both seemed to be holding our breath.

"I have to make this meeting, but can we talk about this later?" I asked. I needed time to let the bomb shell and it's debris land so I could try to make sense of the scattered pieces. She nodded. I couldn't help but pull her in for a comforting hug, not realizing until after it was over that she might not have wanted it.

"I'll call you tonight," she said. "We can arrange something."

So here I sit, in my apartment, the long work day gone, just waiting. I've considered calling her instead and even though I'm exhausted, it is still early. I've considered a lot of things. If there is one thing I have learned from writing my book, it is that no one as strong as her wants to be pitied, so I have erased any trace of that from my mind. I guess I mostly have questions: who is he? How did he come to be in a coma? Was her invitation for me to come to dinner her way of starting to move on?

It is strange how rage and embarrassment can turn on a dime, tumble into a crack in the situation and just fall away. I hear their echos but no longer feel their presence.

***

I feel like I am almost physically causing my characters pain by not allowing their story to continue. I just woke up from a cat nap, and it felt as though Cynthia was tapping from the inside of my brain, trying to burrow out, as though she needed to finish telling her story before she could rest, and since I am standing in her way, she cannot let me rest. If I were being over-dramatic, I would ask myself if am I being haunted by figments of my own imagination. This is just extremely strange, because I don't usually remember my dreams, but this one was vivid, and stayed with me, and doesn't seem to want to fade.

There has been far too much going on in my life to really think clearly about what to do with the lives of fictional characters. I guess I should write at least a little of what they are looking for, to relieve my guilt.

Cynthia decided to stay, knowing that she could always fall back on running if things went awry. She was settling into her surroundings nicely, but every so often she would feel a pull from the part of her soul that loved to wander.

Randell didn't want to keep her against her will, but liked that she was there. He looked forward to their visits, as they were the only part of his routine that weren't just functional: clean the house, clear the lawn, make sure his truck was working, fix things around the property. She almost seemed like his reward, but he kept himself from thinking about her that way. It would be much easier on him when she finally decided to skip town if he didn't care too much.

People change, but he couldn't bank on her changing something that was so ingrained in her nature. He managed his expectations, and loving her made him sit on this precarious wall between knowing that this was just the way she was and hating himself because he wasn't enough to keep her in one place.

~ ~ ~

Randell awoke in the night, his eyes snapping open and scanning the shadows. The place next to him in bed was vacant, but still vaguely smelled of her. He swung his feet off the bed and pulled on the closest pair of pants, to keep the chill of the night air away from his legs.

He heard the sound of voices below, but they were too quiet to hear the precise words. Cynthia belonged to one of the voices. Who was the man she was talking to? Randell slunk closer to the top of the stairs, gaining a view of the shadowy figures in the living room.

"You heard me," the man growled, holding Cynthia close. "We are going to do this together. You owe me."

"I'll help," came her reply. She didn't seem to be in distress; she didn't pull away, but instead seemed to submit to the grasp of this man. Jealousy flared up in Randell's chest. The man was holding her like a lover would. Things weren't as simple with her break ups as she had told him, he thought. Maybe they weren't even broken up.

"He'll never know what hit him. I can clear this whole place out while he's out with you, and he'll never suspect, because he won't be able to find a trace of his things anywhere near this town." The man started running his hand slowly up and down Cynthia's arm. It took all of Randell's mental strength not to leap over the bannister and break those fingers.

"I understand the ruse, Michael," Cynthia replied.

"I knew you would," the man kissed her roughly. "Now go back to bed."

Randell slipped back through the hallway and returned to bed, tearing off his pants and silently tossing them on a soft pile of clothing. He could hear her footsteps gingerly climbing the stairs.

89

He did his best to settle his body in the bed without being rigid. She slipped in next to him, curling onto her side. He thought hard about it before curling her way and pulling her close. She didn't pull away. He didn't know if or when she drifted off, but he was still awake when the sun rose.

If she could plan to betray him, he could do the same.

~ ~ ~

Michael returned to his truck, bundled himself in an old blanket and waited. His recently reworked plan to rob Cynthia's new guy of everything he owned was a brilliant addition to his former plot. He could always kill them later. Cynthia won't see it coming - she was always so easy to control - and if he wanted, he could always frame the guy. That would teach him to take Cynthia away.

Michael slept soundly, secure in his plan. He knew what time they were leaving to go back to town, and would have plenty of time to load up his truck before the guy returned.

~ ~ ~

They were well on the road back to town when Randell mentioned turning back.

"I thought you had everything you needed," Cynthia replied. He had surprised her, and she wasn't a good enough actress to completely hide that.

"I left my wallet on the nightstand," he said. "And you just know that this will be the time that one of those town cops gets on my ass about that busted tail light." He pulled over to the side of the road, glancing at her. He knew she couldn't make a good excuse, but could see her internal wheels struggling to spin.

"Don't worry," he said, pulling her in for a kiss. "There'll still be plenty of time to get you to work."

He pulled the steering wheel around and executed a complicated turn on the narrow road to go back the way they had come. She was still silent, but he could see her growing pale. 'Go ahead and worry,' he thought. She didn't even dig through her bag for her cell phone, probably knowing that it would draw attention to her panic. Good, the bastard wouldn't have any idea that they were coming back.

"Whose truck is that?" he said out loud, pulling around the last corner of his long driveway.

"I don't know," Cynthia stammered beside him. He brought the truck to a stop, blocking the invading truck in.

"You stay here," he said, faking a bit of hostile panic. Well, at least faking the panic - he was finally allowed to show his pent-up hostility. "I'll go check it out."

He slipped from the truck, folded the keys into his pocket and left the door ajar, not wanting to give his intruder any warning. He now had the home field advantage; even if Cynthia freaked out and used her cell phone to call her lover, the ringtone would just help Randell find him faster.

He heard movement inside the front entryway. He recalled the outline of the man from last night as being large, but didn't think he would be much of a match in terms of fitness. Randell crept to the secondary door around the side, and slipped into the kitchen. That's where all the good weapons typically hide in plain sight.

"Who the fuck are you?" Randell called to the man currently trying to unplug his television. The figure flailed slightly, nearly knocking over the television in the process. It wobbled at the edge of the entertainment unit, but stayed upright. Randell strode forth into the room, grabbing a knife from the chopping block on his way. He now blocked the main doors. This jackass would have to go through him or defenestrate himself to get out of the house.

An answer didn't come immediately, as they sized each other up. The guy was a little smaller than his shadow led Randell to believe, but just as soft around the middle.

Michael seethed inwardly, more annoyed that Cynthia had betrayed him for a good set of arms instead of sticking by him like she should have done.

"I'd ask what the fuck you are doing in my house, but that seems a little obvious," Randell gestured toward the television with the tip of his knife.

"She told you, didn't see? That little bitch," Michael spat, dragging his frame taller than his usual stance.

"I didn't tell anyone anything," Cynthia's voice rolled in from behind the kitchen counter. Randell momentarily reflected that she was getting quieter at sneaking around on her tip toes.

"You are with him, aren't you?" Randell asked point blank. He didn't like that his opponents were flanking him. He had banked on her staying in the truck. He pointed the knife higher on the man's body as she came around the counter.

"How could you even ask me that?" she shot back, her eyes wide at the sight of the knife. She moved closer to him, fear all over her face.

I felt myself start to awake through a mental haze. There was something beeping, constantly repeating a nagging tone. I opened my eyes, not realizing I had closed them and drifted off. Eyes still blurry, I answered my phone.

"Hello?" I asked, suddenly checking to ensure I was in familiar surroundings. My living room was dark. A digital clock on my entertainment unit read that it was just after midnight. I gathered that I fell asleep on my couch, after closing my laptop to rest my eyes.

"I woke you up, didn't I?" Gabriella's voice was soft, half apology, half tenderness.

"I don't remember falling asleep," I started. "It's late," I continued, not knowing where to go from there. Figaro peered at me through slitted eyes and promptly returned to slumbering on the coffee table.

"It took a bit of time to build up the courage to call you," she supplied. I momentarily delighted in the role reversal of a gorgeous woman needing to build up courage to call me, until memories of the weekend and our conversation in the stairway flooded back: embarrassment, hurt, a boyfriend in a coma.

"I'm glad you did," I answered, although I was still wary that our conversation would go awry. I didn't know if I really wanted to know this set of details from her life.

"It was a car crash," Gabriella started to explain, jumping right into what she needed to say. I decided it was probably best if I just listened. She spoke of a man she had loved at the time, and how an idiot drunk driver hit him one night while Jack, the man in a coma is named Jack, was walking home from his job. His parents and Gabriella are close, and his parents are keeping him on life support even after all this time, because the doctors are optimistic that he might wake up some day. At least, they had once said it was a possibility, but they made no indication as to how likely it actually was that he would ever wake up. Gabriella used to visit daily, then it became a couple times a week as work became more hectic, then weekly, and now she goes every other Saturday. Last Saturday was her usual visit – the night after we'd kissed.

"I know that the likeliness of him actually being able to hear me is low, let alone that he might understand me," she said. I still pictured her curled up on her couch, but this time there was no wine – just a blanket. "I held his hand and told him about you - about our dinner in my apartment."

I didn't know what to say. I didn't know if I needed to say anything – maybe it was just enough that I was at the other end of the line. I let the silence sit between us.

"He didn't move a muscle while I talked to him," Gabriella continued. "I didn't expect him to. It has been a long time since his body flinched and gave me any hope that his mind was on the other end of the hand that I hold every time I walk in that room."

"I'm really sorry that Jack got hurt," was all I could manage to say. All those months I have been watching her, and I never knew she was grieving. Maybe she learned to suppress it along the way, to ward off the well-intentioned but ultimately unwanted sympathies of coworkers. People can't take pity on you if you don't let them in on the fact that you are hurting. Maybe that is why she was drawn to spending her break times away from the office, and would sneak down the stairway to do so. "I had no idea."

"I know," she replied. I hoped that she was as at peace as her voice portrayed on the other end of the line, but briefly imagined that she might have tears slipping down her face. I didn't want to picture that. "You couldn't have known because I didn't tell you. I don't make a habit of talking about it."

"I can understand that." I felt a pang of guilt for spending the weekend seething in my judgement and anger of her, and of myself. My self-esteem problems forced me to believe that she didn't think I was worthy, because I've spent a lot of time in that headspace and it is an unfortunate default. What happened at the end of the evening had nearly nothing to do with me, not to mention it didn't play into any aspect of deciding whether or not I was worthy of anything.

"I don't really know what the protocol is for breaking up with a man who may or may not be trapped inside his own head," she mused, her voice catching. I felt a wave of vulnerability, and for once, it wasn't coming from inside my chest and attempting to break free. "It isn't exactly his fault that it's been a one-sided relationship since that car hit him."

"Are you seeing anyone, you know, to talk through your survivor's guilt?" I asked, hoping I wasn't getting too personal. At the very least, she needed a friend to talk to about all of this, and although I am a great listener, I don't think I am really qualified to help. Then again, sometimes talking things through is all that is needed, no matter who is listening.

"I've been referred to someone, but I feel silly in going," she replied. I knew the feeling. I loathed the thought of anyone finding out that I see Dr. Macaw, especially people that don't know me well, because I fear being labeled and judged – but I suddenly knew the best way I could help Gabriella.

"I think you should make that appointment," I started, taking a deep breath. "I know you should, because I know how strange it seems to think about sitting in a little room and discussing your feelings with a trained stranger. I know, because I had the same fear, but I have done it, and have been doing it for many months now, and even though I hate thinking that people might find out that I need this help, I wanted to let you know that it really is that – help. No one should be expected to go through tragedy alone, and even though you are a strong woman, there is no shame in seeking out and accepting help." I slowly drew in a deep breath to reinvigorate my lungs after that rushed speech, but held it while waiting for her response.

The other end of the line was silent. I thought for a moment that my phone had died or that she had hung up on me. My lungs began to burn, reminding me that I had filled them to capacity and the air was getting stagnant and superheating.

"Are you still there?" I finally asked, hoping to hear her voice again. I considered for a short time that that admission would have been better delivered face to face, if only to gauge the response in a timely fashion.

"Is that why you started writing again, for the first time since you were a kid?" her voice felt farther away, but at least it was present.

"Yeah, it is. I finally acknowledged that there was something missing in my life, that this omission was making me depressed, and I didn't know what to do about it, so I started to see a therapist." I swallowed, searching for a way to make light of the situation. "I'm sure I can trust you to keep this under wraps, because, you know, I have a wide-spread reputation to uphold."

I could hear the hint of a smile in her voice. "Your secret is safe with me." She paused, and exhaled for what seemed like an impossibly long time. "Thank you for telling me."

"I hope that it helps," I replied, as a thought struck. "In fact, I have a deal to make with you. You can call me for a dinner date once you have made and attended your first appointment." I don't know if I could be called a muse, but I did hope I was a motivator.

She giggled again. I couldn't believe how much I had missed that sound. The slight squeal of joy mixed with a dash of seduction and amusement was enough to make my heart swell up in my chest. Figaro arched his back and pointedly glared my way as he decided to relocate. Perhaps he had heard her giggle and wasn't as much of a fanatic about it as I am. Sometimes I don't understand that cat's taste level.

"You have yourself a deal, Andy," she confirmed, and I could hear her blanket rustling on the other end of the line. In my mind, she was sinking deeper into the couch and stretching out; it was as though her bed was simply too far away, and her current cocoon was too comfortable to consider being transported. I was certainly not one to talk, considering I had recently woken up on my own couch without even knowing I had been asleep.

"I'll let you get some sleep," I said, peeling myself from my own couch, and curling my laptop up in my free arm. My neck was already sore, and if I slept on the couch again, there would be no way that I wouldn't be in agony at the office in the morning. My bed is much more comfortable, and the low light in there from my window makes it relatively easy on my eyes while I type my recollections of our conversation. I've tried to make it a habit of not doing work in bed, but this project isn't technically work, so I bent the rules to fit what I want. To my amusement and surprise, Figaro has burrowed into the covers next to my laptop, as though he is drawn to its heat but not annoyed by the clicking of the keys as I type.

"Thank you for being so understanding about me waking you up," she answered. "I really am sorry about what happened on Friday."

"There is always next time," I declared. "I just want you to be sure that you want there to be a next time. That is all I ask." I would leap at that instant to be in her arms if she wanted me there, but it wasn't my place to decide that. I don't know if I'm being mature about this or if I'm just trying to protect myself. Boyfriend in a coma is a tough act to follow, although I wish I had worded that in a less crass manner.

"I'll let you know after that appointment," she replied. I could hear her voice slipping from this world and into the land of nod.

"Good night, Gabriella."

"Good night, Andy." A faint click, and she was gone. This might have been the first time we bothered with saying goodbye.

I've stayed up way too late recording this, but always want to do it while it is fresh in my mind. I have a decent memory for details, but I'm always concerned slight changes creep into the memories over time. I think I've recorded pretty much everything of importance that was said, and although I am tired, I no longer feel emotionally exhausted. I feel hopeful, but also know that this just may not be in the cards at the moment, and for once, that doesn't feel like a terrible outcome. If we never get together, that will not be a failure on my part – or anyone's part. I have always thought of my past relationships as failures, because I must have done something to destroy them. I'm understanding more and more that sometimes people just don't fit together, and no matter how hard you try, you can't force it. A thought like that would have made me sad before, because I fear that I'll never find a fit. I'm lonely, but some of that is by design. If I want to be around people, then I will just have to face that fear. Right now, I am going to sink into the warmth of my bed. I have a feeling that I will sleep very soundly tonight.

I feel confident that if we are meant to get together romantically, it will happen. I am going to do my best to not push for it. I might, however, have to push my lazy cat over slightly, as he has somehow arrange his tiny frame in a way that takes up all the space in the centre of my mattress.

***

"I told you to stay in the car, but go ahead, lie and tell me that you have no idea who this guy is and what he is doing here," Randell growled. Cynthia stopped, momentarily assuming defeat.

"I didn't want to do it," she started, coming closer.

"Get away from me," Randell spat, directing her with the tip of the knife toward her accomplice. *"I heard you planning to clean me out last night. Now I know you've just been playing me this whole time."*

"That's not it at all," Cynthia tried to explain, but was immediately cut off.

"She made her choice, buddy, so just put down that knife before I take it and stick it in your gut," Michael hissed. He wasn't going to let Cynthia flip-flop again. He wanted the satisfaction of showing the pretty boy that he owned the girl, not Randell.

"I guess you don't realize that I can get away from legal prosecution by saying I was defending my house if I do just that to you," Randell's eyes grew smaller, focusing in a squint directly at Michael. *"It was self defense."*

Okay, I don't know where that came from. I can honestly say I didn't see that threat coming out of Randell, although I can understand how hurt he is, and knew that he would be angry, but didn't anticipate his level of rage. I really don't know where to take it from that exact climax. Maybe I better just leave it for a day or so, and something will come to me.

I can feel Randell pacing back and forth inside my brain, sharpening that horrible knife. Why didn't I even entertain the possibility that he would want to take matters into his own hands? How could I carelessly create a man who is fully capable of murder? Although every guide on writing I've ever read says that you need to input conflict into your plot, I could have picked anything else. I should have made him lose a personal possession that is of importance instead of having him argue with Cynthia and Michael. I don't want him to kill either one of them, but I don't know how to make him stop this rampage to his satisfaction. He's not just fighting with them - he is fighting with me and I don't know if I am strong enough to refuse him what he wants. I don't want to enable this murder, but it is driving me crazy.

I've thought about writing in another character who can save the day; maybe that will stop Randall, and in turn stop his frustrating, fearful presence in my skull. In all honesty, he scares me and I don't know how to control him any more. Choosing to just stop writing his story has me plagued with his terror. I try to sleep but I see his face, just waiting for me on the inside of my eyelids. I sleep out of exhaustion, if I sleep at all. I think people are starting to notice at work, and if this keeps up, I am going to have to take some sick days.

I need to face this fear. I need to finish this story and hope that that gets him out of my head. I need to decide the fate of my characters and follow it through before it breaks me.

***

Maybe I should return some of the calls from Dr. Macaw's office.

I haven't gone to my last three sessions (I've called ahead of time to postpone them all, claiming simple fatigue so as to not alert any suspicions that I am avoiding her - thank goodness for cold season) because I don't want to talk about my failure to just finish this story.

I also don't want the Doc to assume I've gone crazy, considering I would probably be just sleep deprived enough at the appointment to go into a miniature rant about how my characters are trying to murder me from inside my head.

I'm just so tired; I've been working too much.

Rest will make everything much better, if I could just sleep...

***

Gabriella called today. She had her first meeting with her new counselor, and she seemed quite positive about her experience.

"I just wanted to thank you for giving me the push I needed to make the call," I recall her saying. I told her there was no reason to thank me.

I am happy for her but could barely hold up my end of the conversation. I wouldn't be falsely claiming fatigue if I were to give it as an excuse. We made a plan to meet tomorrow night for dinner - and she even offered to cook again, which is good news because my place is a disgrace. At this point, I am already trying to figure out how I can cancel on her without hurting her feelings, because I'm just too damn tired. I can't get this stabbing pain out of my head. I don't think I would be very good company.

I'll wait until tomorrow to make any decisions, one way or the other. Maybe this headache will finally clear up. Maybe I'll be able to get by if I indulge in a little wine - but don't drink too much this time. I think there is (surprisingly) some left from the night of my binge.

***

Dr. Macaw's receptionist was able to slot me in for a meeting today, and both of them even seemed happy to see me. That makes it sound like the Doc is usually grumpy, which is far from accurate, but she just seemed more excited to see me than I can remember her ever being at any previous session. I explained that my voice mail had been on the fritz lately, and that I kept meaning to call back and make a real appointment time but was distracted by my work. We mostly talked about things I made up to cover my ailments of looking incredibly sickly - how I am feeling extra pressure at work, but cannot quite identify where it is coming from. The Doc seemed more relieved to see me, and talk to me, than I feel about the whole situation. I hadn't even noticed that I'm losing weight, and that my face looks gaunt and pale. Why did I go there just to lie? Am I just trying to cover my ass so no one suspects that I'm losing it? Am I losing it? If I am losing it, shouldn't I seek help instead of lying to someone who could help me fix all of this? Is lying the way that the insanity in me allows itself to thrive? Am I truly losing it?

No, no, I'm still here. I can still function. I know what is going on is not normal, but I truly cannot come up with a definition for the word normal anyway. I just have to figure out how to deal with it, and I know that. I just don't want anyone else to jump to conclusions about me. Maybe it doesn't matter. I'm pretty much invisible, most of the time. I'm sure I can go back to that and not draw negative attention in my direction. I just have to get back into the routine of a perfectly sane version of Andy. I'll set timers for when to get up, eat some breakfast - although I now cannot seem to remember the last time I ate - shower, get dressed. I'll try writing the next part of the story in a coffee shop, somewhere nice and quiet where I will be forced to keep calm and just do whatever needs to be done. With all of those people around, I won't be able to worry too much. I'll be forced to keep all of my focus on the page. Maybe I'll find inspiration that can help me resolve this story. Writing from a new physical environment could be exactly what I need.

Before I mainline coffee right into my veins, though, I need some sleep. I guess I should eat, but have no hunger, nor a want to cook. I'll entice myself with something that can be delivered, because my tongue will remind my body how much it loves to eat. I'll eat, and hopefully that will help me to sleep. I'll sleep, and that will help me to get up, go through the morning routine of a sane Andy, and find a coffee shop in which to end this, once and for all. Figaro is starting to give me strange looks for being in what he considers strictly his house during business hours.

This, of course, means I had to cancel on Gabriella. I called her after I got out of my appointment, and insisted that I am coming down with the flu. I hope I didn't disappoint her, but there will be another time for dinner once I sort my life out. She seemed slightly worried over the phone, but I think she knows that I wasn't brushing her off lightly.

I'm officially on sick leave, and I feel like that is best right now. I cannot take the people at work looking at me every time I try to take a walk around the office, as though I am a zombie prowling for his next victim. It's probably because my walk is closer to a stumble, considering how tired I am. I actually stopped my hourly walks over a week ago, but I still feel like people are watching me when I have to get up for legitimate reasons. I don't need their pity. I have never wanted the pity of anyone in my life. I just need to get these characters to shut up and leave me alone. If I had known that this project would be so consuming, I would have happily stayed in the comfort of not trying.

I don't think I am going to love the end result. I know at least one of my characters won't, and I don't think they'll let me make edits. There might not be a happy ending at the end of this book, and I don't understand why I cannot just end it where it is. I'm not writing perfection! Hopefully no one will ever read this story, so why does it have to be complete for them to stop haunting me?

I've tried to stop. I swear I have. I even considered deleting this whole thing, but my head throbs too hard when the screen pops up to ask me if I am sure about deleting the document that I hit cancel just so I can have some relief. The pain never really goes away, and the characters don't fully live on the page - they have made it extremely clear that they are inside my head, eager to immerge.

Sometimes I swear I hear them whispering to me. I'm not crazy. I know this sounds crazy. I think it might be the sleep deprivation, or I might be sick, but I'm not crazy. They are there, talking to me, egging me on and trying to tell me how to end their story. As usual, the ideas I have tried to bounce off Figaro have been shot down. He didn't stop looking smug and evil the entire time I talked to him about this.

I'm glad I never write this pseudo journal when people can see me, because if anyone looked over my shoulder, I'm sure I would be

105

committed. This cannot be the normal novel writing process, if such a thing actually exists. There is no way that hobbits knocked from the inside of Tolkien's head. Stephen King doesn't have room in that skull of his for every ungodly thing he has ever slapped onto a page. I'm assuming that if he had been writing from a loonie bin all these years, instead of his home in Maine, someone would have figured it out and told the rest of us.

***

How did it get so cold all of a sudden? The weather channel seems to think it is the same temperature as it has been for days, but I am nowhere near warm.

Figaro is avoiding me because I try to pick him up whenever he is close just to share in his body warmth. I slept (if you can call it that) with all my clothing on, in my regular sea of blankets, after a mostly hot meal from the takeaway around the corner, but I feel like ice. I've showered and dressed in my warmest clothing, and I can't seem to get my blood flowing. I am tempted to only hit the coffee shop to grab a coffee, but come back home to write, because I don't know if my icy grip can hold my laptop bag right now. It is taking a maddeningly long time to type out these few, short sentences.

I don't feel safe anymore. That feels so stupid to admit, but I can't help it, and I'm really only admitting it to myself. I know I am alone here, but I feel threatened all the same.

I almost feel as though I am being held captive in my own home - in my own head - because these characters won't just leave me be. I really want to do them justice, but they are drawing on so much of my energy that I nearly wouldn't mind being a complete literary hack and ending it with one short sentence. Would that make them get out of my head for good? Will they ever really leave? I could end their existence with a few key strokes - so why do they seem to have such power over me?

***

Gabriella keeps calling, but I haven't picked up because I honestly cannot think of what I would say. I know she is probably just checking in on me, because she hasn't seen me at our work building, but I can't stand the idea of continuing to lie to her and say I'm sick.

At least not the kind of sick that I told her. I'm growing weaker these days, and constantly crave sleep. I just want to curl up and have everything back to normal when I wake up. That shouldn't be too much to ask. I've asked Figaro to sort that out for me while I take care of the napping part, but he never responds to my requests.

I'm not eating well at all. If I wasn't in such a bad state, going to dinner at Gabriella's would be a perfect solution to my recent rapid weight loss.

These characters refuse to be rewritten. I keep trying to go back and edit this document so that things happened differently and they didn't arrive at this critical situation, but every time my fingers go to hit the backspace or delete button, I get a stabbing pain in my head. Every time I try to highlight a paragraph so I can cut it, my fingers fail and I'm wracked with agony. I cannot change what has gone before. I can only move on, but I don't know if I have the strength to do it.

I was foolish to think that I could just write recklessly and clean it up later. That's what they want you to believe - just put something down, it doesn't have to be perfect, and then change it to be whatever suits the story you create. I thought I had finally found a sane way to go about being creative; how is it that I was so wrong?

The more I delay, the more I can feel them taking horrible, long, deep breaths inside my head, just prodding at me to get on with it. Their lungs are superheating the air they steal from me, and scalding my mind. I hope that finishing this story will give me a sense of peace and rest. I see no other way than to continue.

It just doesn't make any sense that I am feeling so much stress over this. They aren't real people, even though they keep walking around my mind like they are more than fiction.

It is time to end this.

***

Michael chose that moment to prove that he could take down anyone who challenged him, and rushed at Randell, aiming his own shoulder into Randell's gut. Michael was slower than his high school football days, and Randell quickly dodged and struck Michael as he was passing with a strong kick to the thigh. Michael toppled, knocking into Cynthia, who was frozen in fear and disbelief. She flew backward, hitting a wall and narrowly missing a window, as Michael tumbled at her feet.

Cynthia's vision began to swim with stars. The back of her head throbbed, and she felt as though the force of the blow had crushed her ribs. She tried to call out for them to stop, but she couldn't collect enough air.

"How dare you come into my house and try to take what is mine?" Randell screamed as Michael picked himself up off the floor and stood in front of Cynthia, not even registering she was there. Michael just wanted to be up before Randell made his next move, and didn't even care that Cynthia was in the room.

"I'm just taking back what is mine," Michael challenged. "With interest."

"Are you talking about her? She's not property, you asshole," Randell raged, gesturing to Cynthia with the tip of his blade. "She's her own person, and you didn't give her the respect she deserves. No wonder she left."

"Yeah, but look at who she's siding with now," Michael spat back, pulling Cynthia around from behind him and holding her firmly to his side. If he needed to, he could use her as a shield, or a way to distract Randell while he got the hell out of dodge.

"Fuck you," Cynthia said through the spinning haze in her head. "Being blackmailed isn't the same as siding with someone."

"Oh, so you are picking this moment to defy me and side with this asshole?" Michael squeezed her tighter. She felt threats emanate from his skin where his body touched hers.

"You are the asshole," Cynthia tossed back, closing her eyes in hopes that the room would be less blurry when she opened them again.

If there was one thing that Michael couldn't stand, it was taking shit from some bitch. He grabbed Cynthia's hair and bashed her face into the television, precariously perched on the entertainment unit. They both fell; it shattered and she landed on top of it, motionless. He barely noticed that she didn't stir; he was used to people learning to just stay down. He was more focused on Randell being distracted by Cynthia's demise and rushed at him again, head on.

Both men crashed to the floor, and the knife deeply sliced Michael's forearm before being knocked from Randell's hand. Michael had the weight, but Randell possessed superior strength. Both had the advantage of rage. They rolled and struck, each of them drawing blood and dislodging items of furniture from their usual places in the living room. Each time they came close to the knife, it was kicked or shoved farther away until they rolled with incredible momentum and the blade ended up flat under Micahel's back. Randell flung his knees into Michael's chest and punched him in the face until Michael stopped moving.

Randell lifted himself from Michael's immobile body and rushed to Cynthia. She hadn't moved at all since the melee began. The pool of blood pouring out over the shattered remains of his television made him pretty sure that she might not move again. He ran for his phone.

"911, what is your emergency?" the woman at the end of the line asked.

"Someone broke into my house," Randell replied, leaning his forehead against the kitchen wall. He recited his address without realizing he was doing so.

"Is the intruder still present?" She sounded almost robotic. Randell knew they had a script, but instead of making him feel calm, it was making him more anxious.

"Yes." He didn't want to be recorded saying that he might have killed him, even if it was self defense.

"Is there anyone injured?"

"I think my girlfriend might be dead. There is a lot of blood." Randell couldn't bring himself to look back at the scene.

"Stay on the line, sir, help is on the way."

A red hot pain flared in Randell's back as he clutched the phone and dug his face further against the kitchen wall.

"She deserved it," Michael whispered in Randell's ear, extracting the knife and plunging it one more time into Randell's torso. He let Randell's weight shift and fall to the ground.

"Sir, are you okay? Sir? Units are on the way. Can you still hear me?"

The voice on the other end of the line kept trying to provoke a response as Michael relieved Randell of his wallet and decided to cut his losses by leaving before someone showed up to help. He had to get his truck off the property before police vehicles from town even made it to the long road to the cabin.

Michael hadn't planned on Randell's truck blocking him in, and couldn't back around it due to the proximity of the house and shed. The keys were nowhere to be found.

"Bastard probably has them in his god damn pocket," Michael grumbled. He turned back. He should have noticed them when he was lifting Randell's wallet, but was distracted by his short time line.

Head throbbing, Michael trudged into the kitchen and barely had time for his brain to recognize the blood in place of Randell's body before his jaw caved in from the force of Randell's bat swing. Both men tumbled to the ground, and Randell just tried to keep his vision from going back. He thought he could hear sirens in the distance, and hoped that that wasn't just his brain tricking him.

So, that's done. It was even more lethal than I anticipated. I suppose it is possible that one of these three people could survive, but I don't think it is likely.

It doesn't feel like a true ending. It hasn't been wrapped up neatly, and nothing has been learned. I think it needs an epilogue - something to give the reader some understanding as to why this horrible situation occurred. As soon as I figure out why, I'll write that. For now, I really need to sleep. I feel like I might actually be able to drift away to a restful dream land and stay there until I regain enough health to continue on in this existence. Sweet dreams.

***

A knock at my door woke me up, but from the extended and rapid nature of the beating, I felt it was safe to assume that the door had been taking punches for longer than I realized. Figaro was already curled in a hiding place beneath the chair in the corner of my room, eyes wide and unblinkingly staring at the source of the booming. I tumbled from my bed, my limbs weak, and wrapped myself in my blanket. The pounding stopped as I shifted the deadbolt and inched the door open.

"So you are still alive," Gabriella breathed heavily, crashing the door open and flinging her arms around my shoulders. I tried to fish my weak limbs out from under the blanket to return the embrace, but she pushed me back into the apartment and moved to close the door. "I've been trying for days to get ahold of you."

"I'm sorry," I started. "I haven't been feeling very well." A tiny jingle of a bell reminded me to close the door completely before Figaro decided to make a run for the outside world. The last thing the apartment building needed was some blanket-clad zombie attempting to corner a cat.

"I know, your office said you are on sick leave, but I got worried when I didn't hear from you for so long," she replied. She was already leading me to my own couch, even though she had never been in my apartment before.

"What day is it?" I asked as she settled me into the couch and made a show of tucking me into my blanket. I saw Figaro's furry face peek around the corner, assessing the situation. I was sure that once he gave Gabriella a status of someone who was capable for putting food in his dish, he would be friendlier.

"Saturday - just after noon." She glanced around. The mess of my apartment started to come into my awareness, nearly blocking the information she just offered.

"I went to sleep Thursday night," I puzzled. "I guess I've started to catch up on my sleep."

"That would explain why I couldn't get you on the phone yesterday," she said, hovering between the nervous energy of being up and helpful, and settling in next to me. My phone's low battery light flicked at us from my coffee table. There is no way I would have heard it from the bedroom, especially not while I was in a deep sleep.

"Sit down, please," I offered. "I can even share my blanket if you aren't afraid of cooties." Being tangled in the blanket made me feel like a child, which would explain my silly vocabulary in that moment. I pulled the blanket from behind my shoulders and flung it over our laps. "I don't think what I have is catching. I'm just exhausted."

"I'm glad I found you," Gabriella offered, sinking deeper into the couch without taking her eyes off me, as though I could disappear at any moment if she wasn't careful.

"Sorry I haven't responded," I said. I looked around the room, the clutter sinking in. "I haven't really had the energy to do much of anything, but I didn't mean to scare you."

"I've spent a lot of time worrying about people who are sick recently," she admitted. "I panicked a little. Good thing your door is tough, and can take the blows." Figaro was now in the centre of the living room, continuing to eye up the creature that was new to his living space. He started to lick his paw and groom his ears, which I took to mean that he wasn't threatened by Gabriella's presence. The loopy, tired part of my brain decided he was try to look his best for the first female house guest in a very long time.

"How are you doing?" I asked, desperately trying to distract Gabriella from my cluttered living room, my more-adorable-than-me cat, and also distracting her from drawing parallels between myself and her comatose boyfriend, since she was now worried about more than one person who is sick.

"I haven't really stopped to think about that in a while," she admitted.

"Maybe you should." We sat in silence while I tried to come up with something to say. "Sorry I had to cancel our dinner - I promise it is just postponed, assuming you still want to do it."

"It would actually help me a lot to make a good meal sometime soon," she said. "I find it therapeutic." She finally noticed Figaro as he began to slink toward her, and didn't seem at all bothered when he hopped into her lap. "When was the last time this cute little guy was fed?" From that moment on, my cat liked her more than me, I am absolutely sure of it. She stroked his head and scratched him behind the ears, and he was one smitten kitten. What a fickle beast he is for turning his back on our friendship in order to win over the affection of this new woman in his life.

Before I could really figure out how it was happening, she was in my kitchen, preparing a shopping list and about to pop out the door to get items she'd need to make dinner at my house. I insisted that she bring me the receipt so I can pay her back, but I have a feeling that she'll "forget". It is simultaneously embarrassing and gratifying to have Gabriella helping me with activities that I can do myself. The least I can do is scuttle around and try to tidy a few things up before she gets back. Doing a load of dishes after I tidy my week's worth of random items littering the living room will be a good start.

* * *

This warm meal feels both foreign and delightful in my stomach. I was able to clean up about half of the anticipated amount of my mess before the cyclone that is Gabriella returned and made a fantastic medley of stew from scratch. I am unsure how she has cultivated so many talents, but I am very glad to participate in the consummation of her culinary creations.

She asked about my novel. "I guess you haven't had any time to really focus on your project," were her words, which made me feel a strange, ironic laughter.

"If I'm honest, I think the novel is the reason I am sick," I chuckled. "I was incredibly stressed out about what to do with my characters, and finally ended it all a couple of nights ago, before I ended up sleeping for a day and a half."

"I've felt pressure when I have a deadline, but never when it is a self-imposed project with an open timeline," Gabriella said, clearing my dishes, despite my protests.

"You've already done enough for me," I claimed, motioning for her to stop taking care of my mess. "I can take care of the dishes later. Rest."

"I can't stay too long," she admitted, finally slumping into the chair next to mine and my tiny, makeshift dinner table. "I've got to leave for business meetings first thing tomorrow because it is a full day of travel to get there for Monday."

"You must really love your job," I joked, knowing she did.

"I do," she giggled. That sound made me wish I had taken up a life as a comedian. "I also don't mind traveling. I really enjoy exploring new locations, or returning to ones I haven't seen in quite some time."

"How long are you away?" I asked, hoping to ascertain when I might be able to see her again. I wanted a chance to have her see my apartment in its usual state of non-chaos.

"I'll be back in time for the next weekend," she replied, standing to gather her things.

"Thank you for the stew," I offered, rising to follow her to the door. "You made enough to feed me for the next couple of days."

"I figured you could use it," she replied, slipping her shoes on, wrapping herself in her coat and checking to ensure she had all the personal items that traveled to my apartment when she came to check up on me. "You are looking a little better already."

"It was really nice to see you again." I only then realized that I was still wearing my blanket as a cape, and felt childish, as though I were a kid being left with the baby sitter who didn't want his Mother to leave. "I promise that my place won't be such a complete heap if you choose to visit again."

"I surprised you, so I can't make any judgements. I'm just glad you are okay." We stood close, neither making a move to leave the moment. Just when I thought she was going to turn and walk out my door, she folded herself into my arms, and I wrapped my blanket cape around her. We just stood there, sharing warmth.

"Enjoy your trip," I said as she slowly pulled away. I returned my cape to the status of cocoon, but kept one hand at the ready to help with the door.

"Get well," she replied. I pulled open the door and watched her disappear into the elevator. I am becoming more and more at peace with the idea that I have no idea where we are going (if anywhere), but trust we'll get to wherever we need to be.

***

I decided to check in with work, and there is nothing pressing that I need to handle immediately, so I made a decision to take another week away. I never use up my vacation time, so I have a lot of banked hours, and I honestly don't feel like going into the office. I'm considering asking to work from home in the future, since the open office layout has always made me feel much less productive than the sanctity of my apartment. I do most of my interactions through emails, and maybe I could convince them that it is in their best interest if I work from home and then only come in on Mondays for the weekly meetings.

The obvious advantage would be that I would have more time to write fiction while between work tasks. I know that would put some pressure on me to get my writing done, or I would become a complete procrastinator and dive into my work (although I somehow think that I am getting better at not doing that). This time away will help me reflect.

The novel isn't finished. I may have fast forwarded to the climax, but I need to wrap it up somehow. It seems disrespectful not to. I'm just not coming up with anything that I feel is good enough to end the story.

Of course, after that will come editing, but I have a strange feeling that I won't be able to change a single thing. I still haven't been able to go back and take out sentences. I have only been able to add to them, but never change the underlying meaning.

At least I have my ability to sleep back. There are no longer any characters stabbing a knife into my brain. Of course, to make that pain stop, I had to stab that knife into a couple of characters.

***

In a classic move of procrastination, I cleaned my apartment today. There is not a room that went untouched. I scrubbed every surface, did several loads of laundry - including items like towels, bath mats, bedding - and every single item in my kitchen is clean and put away. I don't know if my apartment has ever been this clean. I feel as though I am the least clean thing in the entire apartment, but want to leave my shower sparkling for just a little longer before I melt away the layers of dirt that I slowly built up all over my body from the past few days.

It is already past dinner time (I reheated a little more stew while I was scrubbing pots and pans) and I had been hoping to make some progress with the novel. Now I just feel as though sitting in my apartment will make me feel as though I am just watching it fall apart from the incredibly clean state and slowly become the chaos it once was.

I might need to leave the house. It has been over a week since I last left, so it is not surprising that I am needing some time outside of these walls. In the spirits of getting out, but still being both warm and productive, I think I'm finally going to attempt to get some writing done in a coffee shop. At the very worst, I'll be well caffeinated by the time I arrive home and that will force me to stay up and write once I have gotten back into usual territory.

***

My first observation is that coffee shops are much louder than my apartment, however I am finding it very easy to focus in on this page and my fingers are flying across the keyboard. I think I can understand why there are at least a few other people here with their laptops, even though I cannot explain what it is about the atmosphere that makes this activity so focused.

The problem with this focus is I haven't settled on what to do with the story, so I am going to revert to observations until my mind is made up.

I showered before I left the house and stayed under the stream until the water started to get cold. I scrubbed coats of dirt, sweat and grime away from my body, lathered my hair twice, and even elected to shave the strange beard I had started. I kind of miss it now that it is gone, but I know my face will get used to its return to this usual state soon. I was wearing the blanket around my shoulders for so long that I feel slightly exposed without it, but being in a space with other people (and not even more than a handful) is filling me with differing levels of anticipation and anxiety.

I settled on a mocha. I don't understand the differences between all the weird things that you can order as a beverage in coffee shops, but I do understand that this hybrid between coffee and hot chocolate always keeps me warm and is much more pleasant than just drinking coffee (and much less sweet than drinking straight hot chocolate). I was fortunate enough to see someone else burn their tongue on their own beverage moments before mine arrived at the coffee bar, so I remembered to let it cool a little while so I didn't share their fate. I find comfort in learning from mistakes, even when they aren't mine.

I notice that the other people with laptops are younger than I am, but that makes a lot of sense, as they are probably writing papers for school. There aren't that many business people that would take their work to a cafe, I imagine, not that any of these people

122

couldn't be doing business work instead of school work. Perhaps they think I am sitting here, writing a paper on some obscure subject, or a report for a fictional job they have assigned to me in the narrative of their own head. Perhaps they haven't even noticed me at all, as they are far too busy focusing on their own task. I cannot seem to focus directly on my task, but I'm not having much difficulty filling this page with words. I hope that my rambling turns into something of use, although these observations might be excellent subjects to reflect upon for a future project. I believe that I should just write everything down and sort the good from the bad later, if I actually decide to make anything out of this journal that other people might want to read.

Maybe I'll just look at this page until something to say regarding my novel arises. The complete frustration at not letting my fingers type until I figure out what to say in their story might be the kick in the butt I need. If not, there is always caffeine.

***

The room smelled strongly of antiseptic, a sensation that seemed to waft in and out of the nose in a steady and unwelcome rhythm. The monitor beeped somewhere off to the right. It took what seemed like an incredible amount of effort to lift the eyelids, and once they parted, the lashes allowed far too much light into the eyes. It burned. Everything outside of the eye appeared to be differing shades of blinding white. It felt more comfortable to escape back into sleep, as the darkness was warm and protective. The body was bruised and torn, and the mind couldn't take the overload of needy body parts signalling their intense pain. The mind slipped away and blacked out once more, silencing the cries of the body. Time passed, but the mind had no way of knowing how much. Consciousness rose with a new swell of body ache.

"The patient is awake," a high pitched voice muttered, and lab coats rustled in the room. The eyes opened a slit and were once again attacked by the vast whiteness of the room. The tongue parted the teeth and tried to moisten the lips before speaking.

"Did the others make it?" The voice was hoarse and foreign, as though it belonged to someone else and was just borrowed for the occasion.

There was a brief silence while the whiteness gave away to the different hues of a human form.

"I'm sorry to have to tell you this, but you are the only one who survived. What do you remember?"

"I remember everything until I blacked out. Now all I know is pain." The lips were dry again, and the throat ached for water.

"The police will want to ask you some questions, just to get an understanding of what went on," the doctor's voice drifted through the brain haze. Eyelids were manually lifted to check the pupils. "We'll be keeping you here for observation for a while."

"I just want to sleep."

"You can do that, but when you are stronger, there will be some people from the police department here to talk to you."

"What if I don't get any stronger?" The mind didn't really care to get any stronger if it meant continuing to be awake. The mind wanted to sleep until it was all over.

"I'm sure you will. It will just take time to heal your wounds. I can try to help a little more with the pain, but a lot of the work will just take time." The doctor seemed to have pride in her voice that this wouldn't be a difficult process. The doctor wasn't the one in agony.

Then again, the mind wasn't dead, even though it should have died back with the other minds and bodies.

***

I guess someone survived. It felt more natural than introducing another character to the story, just to wrap things up. In fact, I already know who it is that is still alive, I just don't know what to do with them, post ordeal. I don't need to know everything that will occur until the end of their life, but I do need to give them a place to go, so they can stay out of my head. I need to find them a home, because I can feel the drip of their IV in my arm (although I am relatively certain that is the caffeine kicking in).

The last thing I want is to start feeling what my character is feeling, as I imagine the pain is incredibly widespread, not to mention the emotional aspect. I don't want to return to feeling weak and tormented, so I don't know why I chose to leave the character feeling that way. I need to find a positive way to end this suffering, or I may start to share in the misery.

People around me are starting to pack up. Half of my mocha still remains in my cup, long cold and waiting to be finished. I guess the shop is closing now. I did what I could. I made a decent amount of progress. I kind of brought someone back from the dead, but feel as though they might have been more content being left alone. On the one hand, I could have killed them all, but then there wouldn't have been anyone to continue the story. On the other hand, the story is pretty much over, but killing everyone isn't a great ending.

Note to self: next novel, plan things out before you write yourself into a corner. It would feel so great right now to understand where this is going. It would be great to feel that way about anything in life, I guess, but this project already made me terribly ill and I don't want to suffer that fate again. I want to wrap it up, take a really good look at it and decide if it is worth it to edit it, or even show it to anyone. I didn't expect my work to be any good, especially the first creative work in years, but I think every writer secretly hopes that what they are doing is good.

Perhaps I should show it to Dr. Macaw, although I would extract it from this journal first. I don't know why sharing everything with the one person I am supposed to share everything is so scary, but it is right now.

I'm not crazy, and I know that to be true, so I see no need it making someone else suspect anything contrary to that fact. I need to pack up and go home before I am locked inside this coffee shop.

***

I slept well, dressed, and was out the door before my brain really knew where I was going. My feet walked me right back to the same shop as last night. I am very fortunate that the cafe sells a selection of pastries, as my stomach began to rumble as I entered the rich aroma cloud within the cafe and set up my work station.

The more time I spend in this coffee shop, the more I enjoy the outing. I've never felt lonely while sitting at home, but since I am isolated in my individual box, stacked within other boxes, I don't have as much stimulation (besides watching crime dramas, which tend to be detrimental to my productivity, but that isn't what they are for in the first place). Although it sounds natural to rely on imagination to fuel my writing, that doesn't always work if you are thinking too broadly. Try to think of anything - and my mind goes blank. There are just too many options. I need parameters to narrow down about what I am thinking. Now, when I get stuck, I can look around for inspiration.

For example, there is a lady curled up in one corner, still bundled up even though it is a reasonable temperature in here. Her feet are tucked under her, as though touching the floor would force her to seek outside experiences instead of directing her attention to her important task - reading her book. She has one hand wrapped around a very comically large mug, and the other is holding a well-worn paper pack close to her face. Her mug hand alternates between lifting the cup and turning pages, but it always snakes back to the mug as quickly as possible, as though the mug is in danger of slipping away. Her eyebrows are knit together in concentration, and she seems fully immersed in the novel's world. The baristas make loud clashing sounds occasionally, but she never acknowledges them. I think she is only sipping out of reflex, not need for the beverage, as the sips are small and far between. It is as though that action of holding the mug leaves one toe in our world so she stay anchored while she explores the other world contained on the pages in front of her face. Her anchor is tethered to a long rope, and I only expect that she will reach the end of it and pull it tight when she finishes draining her coffee. She's been here longer than I have, so the liquid must be lukewarm by now, but she continues to sip in a slow, steady beat. The end of the cup is the end of her rope, and when it jolts tight, perhaps she'll momentarily realize she's reached the limit of her exploration unless she chooses to jump away from the use of the cup's liquid and just float around her borrowed world, only hoping she will find her way home when the tale is over. She could take the mug with her, as a memory of the world from which she came. The mind is an ever expanding and intricate location to navigate.

The most delightful part of that stream of thought it she has absolutely no idea that her current adventure is fueling, creativing, forming and morphing other adventures that can be taken by other people to other places - both now, in this shared space, and possibly in the future, if anyone reads anything inspired by her presence. I wonder how many people would read that description and fill in details about the world - the smell of roasted coffee beans, the textures, colours and condition of her sweater, the reason she is reading in a coffee shop instead of any other activity. Perhaps she is about to be interrupted by the end of her beverage. Perhaps a friend or rival will enter the scene and engage her in an interaction that will rudely pull her from her fantasy world - and depending on if it is a planned or chance meeting, things could go very differently. The choices of the author can sway things one way or the other, but every reader will absorb the tale a little differently, and spin it around in their own minds to take their own, individual adventure. At best, the author is a tour guide, but cannot control how each traveler seeks to complete their journey. The guide cannot even guarantee that the traveler will reach the end of the journey or necessarily arrive at the exact same destination. A story is merely a loose itinerary of stops that need to happen along the way in order to deliver the message that is bundled together and cast out by the author. It is up to the reader to take that offer and run with it, or do as they please.

Too often, people just follow the narrow course that gets them from the first to the last point, and what they see is a narrow slice of the world around them. A good guide can encourage people to do more than just look left to see the walls of a cultural reference, and I hope to one day be able to create a world so full of meaningful interactions that the reader cannot help but pause to gaze around the sky lines, peek into dark corners and just relish the moment before the action ensues. I know I haven't done that with the current tale, but someone out there might take more out of it than I have intentionally put into it.

What is it about kids (in coffee shops, or the bus, just out on the street) that draws my eye and makes me want to observe every dynamic thing they do? Children are born with the capacity to observe the whole world around them and marvel at what they see, and as time goes on, their view is shadowed and fragmented by learned activities. Things seem impossible when they haven't actually been ruled out; some things just become farther away or feared. Other things are forgotten, as something else catches the eye. Some things just aren't considered, because we haven't explored that area.

Perhaps I see children as being extremely close to the state of being a blank slate. They can become anyone, just like a story can become anything, and it is interesting to see where they are in the journey, and what has brought them there. People seem to think that potential fades over time, but I think it just gets covered up by misconceptions and ignorant judgements. I feel like I am scrubbing away thick layers of grime that have kept me in my tiny section of this enormous world, and am realizing that it is not too late to do what makes me happy. I'm not saying that I am going to start doing things that I've never dreamed of doing as soon as I close this laptop and exit the coffee shop, but I think I'm learning to be more open and less afraid of what is out in the world. Sure, I've felt misunderstood, but I also haven't bothered to correct misconceptions about my nature. I've just hidden behind what other people have said and thought of me, and accepted all of it as things that everyone in the world will think about me.

***

I awoke today and nearly started getting ready for work before I remembered that I am not required to be there until at least next week. I am slowly getting back into my pattern after my stint of obliterated mental and physical health, but I am trying to be mindful of which parts of that pattern I want to continue. Despite all of the stress, this is probably the best project I could have ever undertaken. Instead of jumping into "prepare for work" mode, I took my time and wandered to the coffee shop. This might become a very common place for me to be found. I've never really experienced the feeling of having a location where people grew to know me, but go about their day outside our interaction, only pausing to smile at me (this just happened as one of the baristas asked if I wanted the same beverage as last time). It might be a very small place, but it has a sense of community with which I am not familiar, and am therefore interested to explore. I feel like this is as good a place as any to do some exploration.

Every novel, to some extent, is about self discovery. The whole process of just putting words on the page has reinforced that idea in me. The term "self discovery" seems so weird when you first think of it: self discovery, as though I'm not already an established person who has been "discovered," especially by my own self. Technically, I existed. Technically, I was just living day in and day out, not meandering from the path that was set out for me. Technically, I have done more interesting living since starting this project than I have in the past couple of years. Imagine how much more quality living I can cram into my life if I keep on this road of self discovery. Scratch that - calling it a road implies that it has one set path, when in reality it is more like an entire city of streets, avenues, crescents, culs de sac, and dead ends. Self discovery is more like jogging the same route day in and day out, and then finally realizing that there is another street around the corner and deciding on a whim to change the route and explore what you haven't seen before.

Had I heard this train of thought six months ago, I would have thought that whoever was saying these things about self discovery is a quack, a fraud, or someone who needed to calm down and get a "real job" instead of just trying to give hope to the masses when we all have our place and part to play, and not a large amount of us are destined for greatness. Who is to say that my part to play is set in stone? Can't I understudy a few roles at the same time? Deciding that only a few people are destined to do what they want is erroneous.

It's crap. We might not be great compared to a randomly selected criteria for greatness, but that means nothing. Greatness is something that can only be defined by who is doing it, and if they happen to find others around them who agree, that is a bonus. Sometimes, you find a lot of people who latch onto your definition of greatness, or even people who believe more in your greatness than you do. There are entire sects of fanatics who are devoted to stories that originated in someone's mind, and had the writers not shared them, all of those lives would be a little less great. People wouldn't know what they missed out on, but that doesn't matter. When you find something that resonates with you, and pulls you through a crowd to delight and understanding, you feel that in your soul. Being deprived of that feeling simply because the writer doesn't share their creation is a mind-boggling thought.

I have come to realize that there is no point in doing certain things, day after day, week after week and month after month (much less yearly), if they are not going to be something that either makes you happy or brings you significantly closer to happiness. If you are chasing a carrot that never gets closer no matter how hard you run, then you need to find something that is more attainable. That doesn't mean that the carrot wouldn't have been nice, but it does mean that the carrot wasn't the best choice. The carrot might not be right for you, and you'll be much happier if you accept your strengths elsewhere. It doesn't mean you have "failed" to get the carrot, but rather succeeded in getting what was meant for you.

Reading that makes me feel like someone might take this piece and decide I am preaching that we should be lazy. I am talking about something far from that - no matter what you are working toward, you have to really work for it. To get what you want, you will have to work for it, because there are very few situations in life where exactly what you want is handed to you. Sometimes what you think you want is handed to you, but that isn't the same thing. You will just be working far more efficiently if you decide to work toward something that is good for you and to which you can measure your progress instead of going after whatever people will expect you to want. Don't crush society's carrot. Snack on the fruits of your labour that are enjoyable to obtain instead.

I keep thinking that I need a little time to mull this change over, but the more time I spend away from my job, the less I am inclined to return. I know that I won't be able to leap directly into the writing job of my dreams - hell, I know I might never publish a single thing - but this isn't an either/or situation. There has to be a million more jobs out there that are better suited to me than the one I do simply because I am expected to do it. I want to find something that doesn't make me wince when I wake up and realize my fate for the day is in a cubicle with a bunch of people who do not understand me. I don't know exactly what it is yet, but I do know I don't want to work as many hours, and that I don't want to work in finance ever again.

I will, of course, look at my own personal finances before writing my resignation, but the more I think about this, the more I know it is right for me. I can stay on until they find someone else (within reason - I wouldn't stay on indefinitely). That is the most I can do for them at this point. I want my soul back. They have been using it for far too long, and I need it now. It didn't matter before because I wasn't actually using it. It was like lending out a favourite book - you don't need to have it at all times, but there comes a time when you just need to read it again. I want to read my soul, over and over again, and I don't think I will be able to part with it once it is truly mine again.

So, am I scared about finding another source of income? Yes. But I have a ton of professional experience and skills that are transferable. This isn't my parents' generation where it was incredibly rare to see someone switch careers at my age instead of just working at the same place from teenage-hood to retirement.

This society is much nicer about letting people find their passion. I am going to take advantage of that. All that being said, of course I am still scared, but that is a good thing. If I wasn't scared, it wouldn't be worth doing.

There are things other than working on writing that I want to accomplish, too. It would be ridiculous to assume that I will quit my job and sit down at my laptop for twelve hour days from now until the day I die, just pumping out novels. I'm not even doing that now. I don't write very much in a day, but I am getting better and more disciplined as this process continues. I am also growing to enjoy it more instead of tip-toeing around it, feeling like it is an obligation instead of something I enjoy doing. It is becoming more of a natural habit. I open this document every time I power up my laptop. I'm not saying that I don't get distracted by other tasks (there is a whole internet to explore, after all, even if most of the paths end in cats) but I just feel strange if I don't check in and let my fingers flow over the keys. I'm becoming less attached to the idea that everything I am writing is horrible. I don't think any of it is gold, but the only way to make it better is to keep trying. If I write nothing, then nothing I write can be good. If I write something, I have more of a chance of stumbling on a story, or character, or even setting, that takes me somewhere that interests me. I have absolutely no way of knowing where I will go unless I take the steps to get there.

I really want to share this news with Gabriella. I think I will wait until the end of the week to give my resignation, and then march straight into her office to make sure she is the first person, outside of my coworkers, who knows. And then, I know I will want to celebrate. I'll have to send her a text so I can nail down when she is back in the office, and time it accordingly.

My excitement at this idea is growing stronger and stronger as I type this. I only have the slightest of doubt that I will back down in the final hours, but that is just pure fear talking. I have plenty of time while they are finding someone new to check the personals and start sending my resume off to jobs that are more my speed. I want to work less. I want to be more comfortable. I don't think I could bring myself to be in a corporate culture again. I'll need to find something with even just a hint of creativity in the position. It can even be just adjacent to creative, as long as I get to thrive in an environment that doesn't make me cringe at the thought of getting up and going to the same boring job, day after day until I die.

I have a lot of years to make up for the ones I wasted by doing what was expected of me. Part of me thinks if my folks knew about my career move they would be devastated or disappointed, but when it comes down to it, it won't actually affect their lives at all. This is my life and it is not fair to live it in a way that doesn't make me happy.

I can't wipe this stupid grin off my face, and I honestly don't want to. I am happy. I am regaining my health. I have exciting plans to make and to look forward to, and I have new adventures on which I must embark. For a guy who doesn't know how to spend time on himself, I'm really getting the hang of it. I thought it would feel lonely and stupid and frustrating, but wasn't that my life before I decided to undertake this project? Since when do I care what people around me really think of me? That is none of my business, because there is no one out there who is informed enough on the subject of me to make a valid opinion - and that is partly my fault for not speaking up and telling them who I really am and what I really want. I wasn't even able to tell myself, but I'm learning. I am progressing.

I am ready to make really tough changes because I know they are ultimately good for me, and my position in the company can be filled by someone else. I hope whoever gets the job actually enjoys it instead of smouldering away in silent hatred and suppressed creativity.

***

Another advantage of writing in a cafe like this that I can overhear people talking. Some of these are people who I might never, ever want to have a conversation with in real life, because they sound so completely lacking in personality traits that I would want to associate with, but I can observe how they speak. While looking at these traits, it is hard to not let my mind wander and make stories about their life outside of this moment based on the visual and verbal cues that I have overheard.

There is a woman to my left who is making her daughter sit next to her while the woman sits and has multiple cups of coffee with a friend. This woman is ignoring the time she has with her daughter, and continually criticized the daughter's father, and keeps speaking down to her kid, and other patrons of the shop. The daughter, understandably bored, tried to interject a subject into the conversation so she could be included instead of having to live between these women without saying a peep. She mentioned a sticker on a Mac laptop across the shop, which I have noticed before and found clever. It is of Snow White, having just taken a bite out of the apple that lights up on the back of the screen. The mother looked at it, scoffed, and said, "I hope that is his girlfriend's computer, because why would a guy have a computer like that? He should get a job."

I'm floored by this. I've overheard several subjects of complaining from this table, but it makes no sense to me whatsoever that someone would act this way. Instead of being happy about the fact that it is a beautiful day, or that she has time with her daughter, or showing excitement for the trip that is being planned for next year, she just keeps complaining and putting people - her daughter included - down. I hope that she recognizes her behaviour some day and reflects on it, but it is not my place to judge her life. I only want to observe, and perhaps aspects of her will show up in one of the characters I create in the future.

I obviously know nothing about their lives, but some of the things I have overheard make it seem as though the mother places a lot of blame on her child. That might have made me sad before I started actively observing people, but it creates a whole storyline in my head. I picture that this woman has had a lot of hard times and her outlet for blame is her child - as though she isn't a person who deserves absolutely no blame. She's a child, and not only do kids make mistakes, but all the mistakes aren't entirely their own. Maybe this will transform into a story later, but I think I am a little too annoyed to not keep judging this actual situation, so I'll leave it alone as a story idea for now until I gain a little more distance.

I imagined what it would be like to just tell that kid that I liked the sticker, too. I wouldn't want to do it in front of the mother, and I'm not going to put any energy into trying to have an alone moment with the child, but I wish that she could have that moment of recognition that she's allowed to be amused by things she observes, and not be ashamed of what makes her happy. It is out of my comfort zone, but maybe one day I will be able to interject my thoughts without coming across as arrogant or an eavesdropper. It is none of my business, but I still feel like if I were that kid, I would feel better with some validation and encouragement. I hope she has someone in her life that provides that for her. Too often, we tell people that what they think is wrong without even realizing that we are doing it, and the worst part isn't that they are wrong, the worst part is it is just our opinion that they are thinking or doing something wrong.

This helps sum up a lot of what I feel about my own suppression of creativity.

***

"How are you feeling today?" The Doctor asked, nose deep in his clipboard. He flipped a few pages, and took a few seconds to notice that the patient hadn't answered. "I'm guessing there hasn't been much of a change?" he offered - anything to get a response.

"Why didn't you just let me die?" The patient asked. This hadn't been the first time this question had come up. The Doctor noted that the survivor's guilt was still in full force, and made a note to refer the patient to therapy as soon as they were physically healed enough to be moved. The Doctor was nearing the end of his rotation, and was mentally exhausted, so offering an explanation that would fall on essentially deaf ears was not on his priority list.

"You are going to get through this," The Doctor announced, mostly out of reflex, as he put down the clipboard, checked the bandages over the patient's wounds. The nurses had applied them correctly, so he didn't have to spend longer than absolutely needed with this case before moving on.

"Why me, though?" The patient's eyes turned directly on the Doctor. It looked as though the question was genuine.

"I don't know," The Doctor replied. He honestly never knew how to answer this line of questioning. "But I suggest you make the best of it, and we'll be here to help you do that until you are well enough to leave."

The patient held the Doctor's eye a moment longer, and then tumbled into sleep.

***

I fully know I am teasing the reader here, and I can only hope that I come up with a payoff that makes this section of the book worth reading. It could have all ended in the cabin, but that didn't feel complete. I cannot continue this portion of the book for too long unless the first part was a kind of prologue.

Maybe they are two different tales in the same series, even though the first part is not long enough to be a full book on it's own. I wonder if there is already an established genre of storytelling that is serial short stories (outside of children's literature)? Maybe that is where this piece will fit in.

***

All my silly tales of my antics around the office to keep myself amused cannot compare with how epic today was when I returned to the office. People looked genuinely glad to see me, as people tend to do after an extended vacation. It is that moment of realization that it has been a really long time since you saw someone you once saw daily that flashes in their eyes, and then the reunion slathers a smile on their face and brightens their day with a moment of pleasant association. I saw this pin prick of a moment unfold on several faces as I wandered through the office. It takes coming in after being away to realize that I have been well liked by my colleagues, even if I haven't allowed them to really get to know me. It is hard to introduce someone when you don't already have a firm grip on who they are yourself.

I found myself smiling back and engaging in their questions regarding how I spent my vacation and if I was feeling better; there was a rumour going around that I was really sick - was it true, what was it and am I feeling better? I look better, many people commented. Happiness can do that to a person.

For the most part, when people asked about how I had spent my time away, I spoke in general terms of rest and relaxation. I don't know what prompted me to open up to this one younger lady who must have been the tenth person to ask, but I actually let it slip that I did some work on a creative project while I was recuperating. I don't know if I could describe her look as shock, per say, but it took her a moment to form a response.

"I'm not a professional or anything," I supplied, sorry to have sprung this tidbit on her. "It is just a hobby I'm revisiting." She smiled, and told me that she hoped it was going well. Just like that, someone understood a new piece of the Andy puzzle. I would be lying if I said that it didn't feel great to share that part of myself.

Of course, now that someone knows that I am working on a project, I feel more pressure to finish it, and to do it well, but I have to try to not get ahead of myself. I'm not writing anything for

140

anyone else. I am writing it for me. If I choose to share it later, that is a completely different story.

After making my rounds through the maze of the open office space (not trying to see anyone in particular, but the office is set up in such a way that you almost always have to walk by most of the desks to get to your destination), I marched into my boss's office. He's the type of boss that I can appreciate, because he doesn't micromanage the way I work - most likely because he doesn't really understand what I do and is just content when it gets done - but that also means that we don't really have a working relationship to speak of. I always sense a moment of, "Oh, shit, what is this one's name?" when I know he has spotted me and needs to engage in a polite conversation, such as while we share an elevator ride or get to the appetizer table at the same time during an office party.

"Douglas," I started, knocking on his open door and entering the room a few steps. He looked up from his computer and that moment of name remembering panic flashed through his eyes. When I had first started, that look used to be one of "Have I met this person before?" so at least he had progressed over the years.

"I'm Andy," I jumped in. "From finance." I had no problem helping him out of the hole he'd fallen into. I couldn't remember everyone's names either, although I wasn't in a position of authority over them.

"Oh, yes, of course," he sputtered. I could almost hear the cogs in his mind spin into action and gaining momentum as he recalled information that he knew about me in order to make a response. "You've been out for a couple weeks - I almost didn't recognize you."

Either my time away was even better for my health than I thought, or he was a master of covering up his memory gaps. "Yeah, I had some vacation time saved up, and took some sick time."

"Everything is okay, I presume?" he asked. Something I liked about him is when he spoke to anyone, he did give them his full attention. It didn't translate into a long term memory of your interactions, but I can tell that he actually cares about the people under his employ.

"I'm feeling better," I admitted, "but that is something I need to talk to you about. I haven't felt this good in a very long time, and a lot of it has to do with the fact that I wasn't in the office over the last couple weeks. I'm discovered that this environment isn't one in which I thrive, and I've decided to make a life change."

"You're leaving," he guessed, a look of dismay in his eyes. The pessimist in me could see him starting to wind his cogs in the direction of trying to figure out how to find someone to replace me.

"I am," I offered. "However, I understand that this puts the company in an awkward place, and I have decided to stay on until someone is found to replace me - but I want to do so on my own terms." I had his full attention, and started to outline the process I had created. He could go right ahead and put up advertisements for my position, and once he had candidates that he thought would do the trick, we would interview them together. "I know that it can be hard to judge who will do a job well that you yourself don't know how to do," I remember slipping in. It wasn't a judgement or an insult. There are very few people that understand the ins and outs of my boring but complex job.

"Until someone suitable is hired, I'll stay on, but I want to work from home," I stated. I was adamant about this fact. I surprised myself with how ready I was to stand my ground on this point. As much as I got nostalgic while walking through the office and being greeted by people who are honestly nice, working in that environment day after day was not something I wanted to inflict upon myself.

"Would you consider staying on if you could continue to work from home?" Douglas asked. He wasn't begging me to stay - it was a simple question to help him in understanding the situation.

"That is something I could do for a while, I think," I answered honestly. "But I would want to work far fewer hours, and I would want to be more of a consultant instead of doing 'make work' tasks to fill my time."

"You've put in an amazing amount of work into this company, Andy," Douglas replied. "I would like to see you stay on, but I know I cannot stop you if you aren't happy here."

"It's just not for me anymore," I said. "Everyone has been great, Douglas, but I need a change. I'm looking forward to it."

"I want to support you in that, Andy," Douglas said, rising and putting his hand out to shake mine. "Let me know what you need. I think we can arrange a system where you work from home, and I would be delighted if you would help groom a replacement." He chuckled. "You are right in that I don't know how to replace you - I'm not a numbers guy."

"As it turns out, neither am I." I turned and walked away from the job that I thought would take me into retirement. I guess I will keep some of my job security, and I might be able to pull in a salary that is relatively close to what I am used to earning but with far less work and no time in the office.

I left his office feeling invigorated. Before beginning this project, I never would have imagined that I could get exactly want I wanted and needed simply by asking for it. Putting my needs out there always seemed selfish, and against the terms of employment. I've never been one to really go against the grain, but I'm learning to accept that aspects of me are part of my whole being, and they shouldn't be hidden.

It felt like I was strutting as I made my way through the maze of the office toward the semi-secret staircase. I have no idea if I looked different to anyone going about their business, but I felt different. I felt more confident. I felt closer to the Andy that they assumed I might be based solely on the name my parents gave me - minus the party boy antics. I slipped up the staircase and into Gabriella's office. I had never been there, so it took a little while to find her niche.

"I would like to take you for lunch, when you are free for a break," I said, tapping her on the shoulder. Her face erupted in a huge smile. We haven't seen each other in about a week, and the last time she saw me I was in a blanket cape. She looked as gorgeous as she always did.

"It is so good to see you among the living," she said, wrapping her arms around my neck in a tight hug. "I have a couple of hours of work to get through, but I can meet you in the lobby at noon. Does that work?"

"Sounds perfect," I replied. "I have news to discuss."

"Have you finished your novel?" she guessed, releasing me to look at my face.

"Not yet," I admitted, completely unashamed. That is going to take some time. "I'll tell you over lunch." Not wanting to give anything away, I turned and walked all the way down to the lobby via the semi-secret staircase.

I've been sitting in the lobby for over an hour, just pecking out this tale and watching people come and go. I am the most calm I have ever felt in this building. I feel an incredible sense of relief and peace. Sure, I might not make as much money from here on out, but I'll get by. Sure, I might not actually write anything worth publishing, but that isn't the be all end all thing to do for a creative person. I don't need the world to know what I have written, but I do need to write it.

Gabriella should be down for lunch any time now, so I'm going to pack up and just enjoy the people passing through the lobby without the protection of being behind the laptop. Perhaps I'll find another person to base a character on, or someone to describe and ponder. Perhaps another chapter will unfold while I wait.

"Do you know why you were referred to me?" the Shrink asked. The patient guessed that this was something they always asked so they could get an understanding on the current mental state of their "guests".

"Yeah, don't worry, I know that I'm a little fucked up and that concerns people," the patient replied.

"Anyone who went through what you did would be in a state of emotional turmoil," the Shrink supplied. "You must know that this is considered a normal reaction, given the circumstances."

The patient briefly considered a retort about the situation in question not being a textbook case, but decided to clam up instead. They sat in silence.

"Do you want to discuss the events of that night?" The Shrink asked, laying her notepad aside on a small table. "Talking through it can help some people release it and move on."

The patient pulled in a deep breath, which stabbed at their lungs. "Why aren't people who have suffered 'turmoil' allowed to just forget about it?"

"That's not the way the human mind works," the Shrink explained. "You might think you have forgotten it, but it stays with you."

The patient pondered this. The Shrink let the silence hang for a while.

"You can speak in as many or as few details as you want. Whatever makes you the most comfortable. If you are willing to speak about it, I might ask questions, to clarify my understanding and to figure out how certain things made and make you feel. Is that something you think you can do?"

The patient sat in silence, replaying the events of that day in their head. The Shrink waited. She knew that it was enough to just be in the room while a patient processed events and feelings, and if she pushed too hard, they might never open up. The rest of the session passed in silence.

***

"It's been eating at my mind all morning," Gabriella bounded up to my cosy spot in the lobby. "What is your news?"

"I've decided to quit my job and spend more time writing," I replied, rising to meet her. "I'm going to help Douglas find a replacement, stay on and do some consulting work, but I no longer have to report to that office." I pointed upward, as though the office was just above my head.

A wave of emotions passed over her face so quickly that I didn't have a chance to decipher them before her arms were slung around my neck. She held me tight. I held her back. I didn't know what was going through her mind until she pulled back and started to talk.

"Your soul is going to be a lot happier," she started, smiling widely. "This is a really brave move, but I think it is going to work out really well. Even though," she teased, "I won't haven't anyone to eat lunch with anymore."

"There's no rule that says I can't drop by every once in a while to have lunch with you," I pointed out. "I know that when there are huge life changes, people say that things will stay the same even though everyone knows that is bullshit. This won't be the same," I gestured between the two of us. "But it will grow, if we want it to."

I didn't see it coming. I don't know if she saw it coming, either, but she stepped into my personal space and kissed me, in front of the entire lobby. I have no concept of how much time was experienced while in that kiss, but it was exciting and an enjoyable surprise. She pulled away, blushing slightly.

"Where would you like to go for lunch?" I asked, taking her hand in mine and starting out the front door, attempting to not gauge the faces of the people around us. I don't care how anyone else felt about that kiss besides Gabriella.

"Wherever you want, as long as they serve food," she replied, allowing me to lead her.

We shared giggles, smiles and some delicious finger food at a nearby restaurant and chatted about my newfound freedom and her recent trip. For the first time, I wasn't experiencing a jack hammer of anxiety in my chest, and just slipped into natural conversation between bites. It amazes me how much this one change in my life is spilling over into other aspects of my life. I'm looking forward to completely embracing this change. Even my fear about it has receded, as though it was a jacket that I took off and left in Douglas' office. What I formerly thought was a jacket of security against the weather of the world was largely made of fear, and I don't want it back. Part of me knows that I am going to get scared again, but I just need to remember to unwrap whatever is causing my stress and discard it.

After dropping Gabriella back at the lobby of the building where I am only technically still employed, I sat down and wrote Douglas an email, thanking him for his understanding, but I am staying true to not wanting to return to that environment upstairs. I let him know that I'll be up next week to clear my desk of anything that is actually mine and go over any candidates that he might be able to find by then, but any tasks he needs done can be emailed to me and I'd create invoices for my time.

Hitting send was a huge sigh of relief. It was still early afternoon when I left the building and allowed myself to walk home instead of use transit, simply so I could take in the surroundings at my own pace instead of working in someone else's schedule. I know it is something that works for most people - or that most people can adapt to - but I am looking forward to scheduling my own time. It is going to be a strange change, but I am breathing more deeply knowing that I am reopening potential that I had assumed was lost. It was really just ignored.

***

The pain was rising again. The drugs never lasted long enough to take it completely away, but the patient would be appreciative if the pain didn't go from dull to splitting so quickly. The Doctor wouldn't prescribe something stronger for fear of a dependence. "I would probably take it all at once anyway," the patient mused.

"Your papers are done," the Doctor said, strutting into the room. It was a different doctor than usual, but the patient couldn't remember names anyway. "I'll assist you to the entrance. Do you have anyone coming to get you?"

The patient bit back bitter words of not having anyone who would do that if they asked. The Doctor didn't need to know that. The patient had always been a loner, anyway.

"I'll be fine, Doc, just glad to get up again, even though the pain is killing me," the patient replied, trying to just get the ordeal to finish.

"That will get better as your body heals," the Doctor reassured. "You have your prescription, and you can call the help line if you have any questions." It sounded rehearsed, but then again he had probably said it over and over again since beginning his career, so it was routine to him even if it wasn't to his patients.

There was a look in the eyes of every person the passed in the hallway on the way to the exit that was strong and recognizable. The patient had heard that the case was big news, so this wasn't a surprise. It was, however, an unwanted draw of attention.

"Any parting questions?" the Doctor asked, parking the wheelchair just outside the sliding doors and preparing to help the patient disembark.

"Doc, if you were in my shoes, would you cut and run, or would you stick around and live where everyone knows the worst part of your life?" The patient hadn't planned it ask this question, but it was bobbing around the mind.

The doctor paused. This wasn't something he'd ever been asked, and the patient became more human in his eyes - not just a tough case, but someone who needed an honest answer.

"I, well," he started. *"Can I answer completely off the record, as though I'm not a medical Doctor giving advice to a patient?"* The last thing the Doctor needed was a malpractice suit for giving advice that a patient genuinely asked for.

The patient perked up - a real answer was not something that was expected, but something the patient looked forward to.

"Yes," the patient answered. *"I'll treat this as though we've never met, and it is just a question posed to someone who has heard my story."*

"In that case, I would do the opposite of what you've done all your life - whatever that is. This near death experience is a reason to completely change the way you do things. I'm a firm believer that when things get incredibly tough, that means there is a tough change that needs to be made. Which ever option - cut and run or stick around - is harder, I think that is the one that you need right now. Take it as a sign from the universe, or just a luck of the draw, or the word of God - whatever appeals the most to you - that this is your chance to move on from whatever is not working in your life." The Doctor paused, looked at the patient in the eye and smiled slightly - not his usual professional smile, but the one he reserved for interactions that meant more to him than those in his routine. *"That's what I would do, anyway - if things got really bad for me."*

The patient pushed against the armrests of the wheel chair and slowly rose out of the seat. The arms were shaky, but that would fade. The torso was tender, but that would fade, too. *"Keep* the good and discard the bad," the patient mused. "Thanks Doc, it was good to hear an honest answer." The patient looked him in the eye - no pity there. That was a look the patient could get used to.

"Do you need me to call you a cab or anything?" the Doctor asked, slipping back into the routine of patient release. The patient tapped on pockets and lifted their bag, making sure all the relevant person articles were in place.

"No, I can take it from here," the patient replied. "I've decided what I'm going to do."

The Doctor watched the slow pace of the patient until they disappeared down the street, and sighed before turning the wheel chair around and taking it back into the trauma ward. The image of that weak pace stuck with him until a new case was handed to him. He was confident in his advice, but knew he couldn't do anything more unless the patient waltzed back into the hospital. He exhaled the experience and breathed deeply into the new case.

~ ~ ~

"How can I help you?" the clerk behind the counter chirped cheerily.

The former patient hoped they were covering their injured gait enough that people wouldn't notice unless they really examined the pace and movement. A bulletin board advertised several services - pet sitting, haircuts and moving services. The former patient pulled on a tab, glanced at the map next to the clerk's desk and smiled.

"I'd like a ticket to the farthest place from here that the bus travels," the former patient indicated, tapping the map but not bothering to read it.

"You're in luck," the clerk chirped. "That bus is just about to board. It's a long trip, though, so I hope you have something to keep you occupied."

The former patient pulled a random paperback book from the rack next to the desk and slapped it down on the desk. "I do now," came the reply. The clerk seemed to have mastered the upsell. The former patient couldn't remember the last book they read; they'd recently heard that sometimes it is good to try new things.

"Are we running this on a card or cash?" the clerk asked, ringing up the total. A card appeared on the desk and the interaction was over in a matter of seconds.

"Can't back out now," the former patient thought.

"Here is your ticket, don't forget your book, and have a great journey," the clerk chimed, pointing toward the appropriate bus.

The patient boarded the bus, settled into a seat in the back, cracked the spine of the paperback and never returned to that town ever again.

***

It feels oddly relieving to be finished that story. I think I was starting to get anxious about my character again, and I can actually feel them at rest now. I think the ambiguity leaves this tale open to fit the needs of whoever is reading it, although I know who the former patient is, at least in my own mind.

I'm looking forward to just letting that story rest for a while. I'd like to revisit it later, but taking a break from it will be a weight off my shoulders.

I've never experienced the common phenomena, but this might feel similar to living with a child and then having them leave the nest. It obviously hasn't been the same length of time as raising a child, but there are some parallels that can be drawn. Stories are the children of the author, but they become their own entities and go out into the world, changing the course of other people's lives along their way. I've influenced the story as best I can to be a positive entity, but those exterior interactions are out of my hands.

I'm also feeling a sense of pride. I might never been a parent to a human - I'm a little old to start now, although I won't rule it out - but I can be the creator of countless characters and stories. That is a refreshing thought. I have much more control over my life and what I do with it than I have felt in the past.

I had an appointment with Dr. Macaw today, and even though I've gone back to enjoying our meetings (instead of dreading them and hiding aspects of myself when I did bother to attend), I think I have progressed to a point where I don't need them any more - not on a regular basis anyway. She was highly animated about my progress, which I suppose was an abrupt change to her because I went so long between appointments. She said something to the effect of she wouldn't have thought I was the same person if she didn't see it with her own eyes. I think she was mostly joking when she mentioned using me as a case study for finding confidence through creative release, although I would be willing to talk about it if it wasn't on my own dime. I feel like I have slightly misrepresented my process, since I hid that scary section of time from her (when I became incredibly ill), but I can try to explain that if she really wants to know.

I am enjoying picking where to set up my "office" each day. I have the freedom to stay at home or hit my local coffee shop. I can go basically anywhere that provides wifi, although I only really need that to check emails or distract myself. The bigger factor is finding a place to plug in my computer, in case I decide to camp out for an extended period of time, but I have already claimed a favourite place in my coffee shop that allows me to achieve this.

This is one of my most important strategies at the moment - not anything to do with finance or the company or numbers, but where I can be comfortable doing what I want to create. I'm just letting that sink in a little. It feels really good. I know I should be more eloquent about it, but I just want to revel in the thought instead of try to explain it too much. I feel happy. I feel content. I still have anxiety about certain aspects of my life, but now that I have a firm handle on this feeling, it is much easier to return to it when I start getting anxious.

Something Dr. Macaw suggested was finding someone to read my story once I finished it. I don't even know how to start with that, besides allowing Gabriella to read it because she is curious. Maybe starting with a friend is the way to go, because stories aren't meant to be contained. I'll give her the option of reading it tonight, but I'll need to extract it from this document first.

***

"But who lived?" Gabriella asked as she put down the pages. She hadn't said an actual word the whole time while reading the story, although I stealthily watched her reactions and was amused by the small sounds that slipped through her lips. I was nervous about her reading it, but also knew that even if she thought it was the absolute worst thing she had ever read, she wouldn't storm out of the apartment (or kick me out, considering I had brought the story to her apartment and worked up the courage to hand it to her after dinner).

"Who do you think lived?" I replied. I was interested to see how she achieved her conclusion based on what was written in the story, and what could be inferred. I have no idea if I was completely clear, completely vague, or where on that spectrum I should consider the ending of the story. It is hard to judge when I already know that outcome.

"Well, I guess it depends on who you are rooting for," Gabriella started. "If you really want Randell to finally move on from the town that has basically imprisoned him for his whole life, then you hope it was Randell. If you are hoping that Cynthia made it, it feels like she completely disregarded the Doctor's advice and kept to what her pattern has always been, which goes to show that people don't change. It all depends on what message you want to get out of it."

"Who's to say it wasn't Michael?" I kept my face as neutral as possible.

A comically horrified expressing clouded her usually serene face. "You have got to be kidding me!"

"I didn't say that was the answer," I chided, amused at her outburst. "I just mentioned that it could be an option."

"Michael wouldn't show the regret that the survivor did," Gabriella replied, further proving to herself that the bad guy could not have triumphed.

"Which do you prefer?" I asked. I could tell she wanted me to give her the answer, but I preferred to watch her puzzle through it. She was technically correct in thinking that there is no right answer. I don't know if that makes my story better or a cop out, but I really like that aspect of it.

"I prefer that Randell got out of dodge," she replied. "People can take control of their lives if they really want to - they just have to be made aware of that option. That way, the story is hopeful. It doesn't really matter where he is going, because the act of leaving in itself is a victory." She looked at me, expectantly. I did my best to keep my face neutral. "Damn it, you aren't going to tell me for sure, are you?"

"If you have already figured it out how you like it, what does it matter which way I say it ended?"

"Because you wrote it!"

"Just because I happened to type the words into a document and then print them on a piece of the paper doesn't mean that I have complete control over the story," I replied. "The story, in its individual form, belongs to whoever is reading it."

"Are you saying you are completely okay with people deciding that it ended differently than you intended?" she asked. I could tell she was trying to back me into a logical debate so she could ascertain my intended implications. I was ready for this.

"Who says anyone is wrong?" I answered. "A series of events is different depending on who you are in relation to those events."

"Yeah, but doesn't the reader's role in the act of reading stay the same from work to work?" I didn't want to think of what happened next as me trying to convince her or win the argument, but an idea popped into my head.

I pulled the pages from her fingers, sorted them in order and put them aside.

"Can you do me a favour and tell me about the dress you wore the first night I was here?"

"Why are you changing the subject?" she giggled, reaching for the pages again.

"Just humour me?" I hoped I had picked something that would help her see my perspective.

"Well, it was one of my favourites, this royal purple satin weave with princess seams and a modest but not frumpy hemline. Is that what you wanted to know?" Her eyebrows knit together and sheltered her eyes as they searched my face to see if she was giving me want I wanted.

"What you've just told me is influenced by who you are," I started. "You look at how a piece of clothing is made, and what it is made of, whereas I just knew it looked nice on you, and wondered about where it came from - because that is my view point."

A spark flew up into her eyes. "So you are arguing that the person reading something influences the way it is read?"

"Exactly." I made a note that her phrasing summed up what I was trying to convey nicely.

We sat in silence for a moment as I tucked the pages into my laptop bag.

"Our whole lives are lived through perceptions, observations and reactions. How each story continues or ends is influenced by every element - how it is communicated, who created it, who experienced it. Sure, I would be mad if someone just took my words and claimed they owned them outright and somehow profited from them, but I have no problem with however people choose to receive the words." I chuckled, and coughed to myself. "Obviously, I would prefer that the story be perceived as being well written or well told, but that is a matter of opinion, and I can't expect everyone to share that opinion. I can't even expect one human to have that opinion, but I learned a lot while writing it, which in itself made it important."

"Are you going to choose to share it?" she asked, noting that I had tucked the pages away.

"I already chose to do that," I answered, smiling at her. "I could have just left it in the original document and walked away from it."

"That wouldn't be fair," she mocked. "Doesn't it make sense that the muse should get to read the word she inspired?"

"That does sound ideal, but the woman who inspired the character of Cynthia, chances are, will never read this. And if she did, she might not even recognize herself in it, because I made observations of her for a brief time and created a character. Chances are that character isn't anything like the woman I saw briefly in that food court. Plus, elements of the story were influenced by observations that had nothing to do with her."

"I guess you are right," Gabriella conceded. "It would be kind of strange to track her down and tell her that you wrote her into a story and then killed her."

"Or not, depending on who reads the story," I smiled.

She sighed in exasperation. "You really aren't going to tell me."

"You already know; my personal opinion shouldn't influence yours just because I wrote it down."

"I just want to be right." She rose and moved toward the kitchen to refill our glasses.

"No matter which way you decide, you are right." I knew that would irritate her, but it was true.

"Well, let's drink to doing what is right, then," she announced, returning with both of our glasses filled high.

"To doing what is right," I replied, clinking my glass with hers. We sipped, looked into each others' eyes and enjoyed the silence as we enjoyed the mixture of flavours and aromas from our wine glasses.

I made a decision. I took her glass with my free hand, placed them both goblets on the coffee table and moved closer toward her. I took both of her hands in mine, studying the joints of her fingers and each ring that wrapped around her digits. When I was ready, I looked into her eyes and leaned toward her -

What happened next? You can decide that for yourself, Dear Reader, as I feel like I have shared enough of my personal life with you. Did the guy get the girl in the end? Does it really matter? No matter where a story stops being recorded or told, that doesn't mean it is the end. I'm still living on after that moment. Sure, my life is influenced by what happened in that interaction. I am influenced by all of the events of my life: how they made me feel and how I reacted to them. Does it matter what happened? To me, it does. You might even feel attached to what the outcome was. I did kind of leave it at a cliffhanger, for which I am only partly sorry. It is my hope that when you finish reading this document, in whatever form you have acquired it, that your biggest impression isn't that it didn't end; no story ends, the events just stop being recorded.

The only absolute end for the body is death, and I can assure you that that was not what happened in that moment in Gabriella's apartment, but even if it did, the soul can live on if it has been interwoven with enough other souls. If this were a tale told by a different teller, different details about what was going on in the world would be offered. I've recorded what I can, but choose to stop the record of events to prove my point. It doesn't matter how that evening ended, because no matter what, that moment could cause an infinite number of reactions. You can choose your favourite, but I've chosen to keep that moment private.

If you aren't too angry with me, though, I'd like to leave this parting advice: really pay attention to the stories in your life. They are everywhere, and they are powerful. Some are meant to amuse, some are meant to make you think, and some are not meant to be anything more than what you want them to be. If you don't like a story in your life, don't accept the recorded end as the last event - keep living the story and change however it currently fits into how you want it to be. I wouldn't have written this if I listened to the characters in my life who said it wasn't possible. Be mindful. Be present. Be what you want, and keep creating your own story.

Author's Note

Thank you, Dear Reader, for taking the time to (hopefully) enjoy my first novel. Having people read my work means a lot to me. Please reflect on my words and, if you choose to do so, take those that are useful with you when you put this book on your shelf and leave it to collect dust. Think, feel, challenge and engage with people and characters in your life, because we can be captured by the stories we tell, or we can be happily enthralled by them.

I'd like to thank the first folks to skim my pages; these people helped point out a few of my thousand typos and their kind words of support gave me the courage to publish: David Creighton-Offord, Chad Weber and Wendy Morin. Thank you all so much for taking time to tumble through the world I created.

Kathy Trithardt

28156645R00096

Made in the USA
Charleston, SC
02 April 2014